STATE OF THE *Heart*

ISBN: 979-8-9996017-0-4

Cover design by Ivanna Nashkolna
Edited by Grace

Printed in the United States of America
First Edition: 2025

For anyone trying to find themselves.

STATE OF THE *Heart*

CHAPTER 1

Every point of entry is heavily guarded. Or, the way I see it, every possible exit is being blocked.

Men—and a few women—stand in crisp, tailored suits, trying to blend in. To a casual observer, they might pass as distinguished guests. But to anyone really paying attention, their stiff postures and constantly sweeping gazes give them away. Years of intense training have taught them how to look polished, not invisible.

I'm at a charity gala my mom is hosting. But it's not just any charity gala. This one's a national spectacle. The kind of event that attracts a flood of politicians and foreign dignitaries every year. Think the Met Gala—but for world leaders in overpriced suits.

I scan the room, watching a sea of high-powered schmoozing unfold. Every conversation feels like a political campaign. Near me, a woman pouts like a spoiled actress, whining about how her husband "had the audacity" not to buy her a purebred pony. Apparently, a half-bred just wouldn't do. I stopped listening halfway through her dramatic speech about how she'll be the laughingstock of her riding club because of it.

I stifle a yawn and try to focus on the small group around me, but my mind is already drifting.

"Ah, tired already, Miss Hastings? It's not even eight."

The white-haired gentleman—Senator from Minnesota, I think—winks like we're sharing some private joke. I offer a polite, fake laugh, just convincing enough, before shifting my attention to the Senator from Arizona. He's in the middle of a long-winded story about his golf handicap.

I can't take it anymore.

This room is packed with people who are not only decades older than me but also seem locked in a competition to prove who's richer, more powerful, or more important. Not all of them are like that, sure, but when you cram a bunch of elite donors and politicians into a room, the unspoken one-upping practically buzzes in the air.

I reach up and toy with my diamond earring, a signal I've prearranged with my partner in crime. Somewhere in this crowd, he'll see it and know: it's showtime.

As I lower my hand from my ear, I casually cover my mouth with it—an attempt to look like I'm about to lose the appetizers I've been nibbling on all evening.

"If you'll excuse me," I say, stepping away from the small group and heading toward one of the heavily guarded doors.

"Sweetie, are you okay?" Mom steps into my path, her

long silver dress twinkling under the harsh lights of this stuffy room.

"I'm fine, just a little nauseous. I'm going to run to the ladies' room for a minute," I lie, needing an excuse to disappear.

"Hey, Princess, what's going on?" Dad appears beside Mom, slipping an arm around her waist and pulling her close.

I press my hand over my mouth, stifling the urge before hurrying past them toward the door. A guard shoots me a concerned look, as if I might throw up on his perfectly polished shoes. Keeping my hand pressed to my mouth, I rush down the hallway, passing several guards stationed along the way.

I push open the door to the ladies' room, glancing under each stall to make sure I'm alone before dropping my hand from my mouth. I pace the length of the small bathroom several times. Then the door creaks open. I catch my reflection in the mirror — red hair half pulled up, sparkly pins holding the rest in place. My dark green A-line dress has a full tulle skirt, covered in glittering flower embellishments. It's beautiful and elegant, sparkling under the lights — but I'd rather be home in my sweatpants.

"El? You in there?" a posh accent calls from outside the door. I say nothing. I hear him warn someone behind him not to come in. Then a head of perfectly styled dark blonde hair peeks around the doorframe. I stop pacing and stare wide-eyed into the calm blue eyes of my best friend. He steps inside, leaning against the door with a smirk that says he knows I've been panicking.

"I may actually be feeling a bit nauseous, Ollie. There's no way we can pull this off." I keep pacing.

"No, we're doing this. No backing out." He steps closer, hands firm on my shoulders. He breathes deep, silently urging me to do the same. "That's right, in, out. In, out. Come on, Els, we need this, even if it's just for an hour."

I take another breath and nod. He's right — of course he is. That's all we want, a taste of freedom, just a moment not under constant surveillance.

"Ready for part two of the plan?" he asks. I nod again, bending down to slip off my nude heels.

Ollie shoots me one last look, like a silent triple check, before turning toward the bathroom door and cracking it open just enough to peek out.

"James, Eleanor's a bit sick with her, uh, monthly visitor. Can you grab her the needed products and…" He steps back in, smiling at me. "What meds did you want? Tylenol? Benadryl?"

I give him a look. "Yes, please get me allergy medicine. No, you weirdo, some Midol."

He peers back out the door. "Some Midol, as well as peanut butter M&M's." Behind his back, he flashes hand signals at me—

A two. A five. A two and a fist.

What on earth is he doing? We never agreed on hand signals for this plan. I don't understand a word of it!

"Oh, and James, be sure they're the peanut butter M&M's, not any other kind."

No reply from the other side as I keep my eyes on the back of Ollie's head. Then he starts a countdown with his hands—now I get it.

Three.

Two.

One.

He draws back and grabs my hand before throwing the door open. We don't run—that would draw immediate, unwanted attention—but we move quickly, knowing our window is tight. Down the hall, a security guard steps into view.

We stop. I recognize him instantly—Marks, head of my security team. Ollie sees him too and presses me against the wall, nuzzling his face into my neck as his arms wrap around my waist, pulling us flush together. Marks eyes us, then he shifts his gaze away. He stops a few feet down the hall, close enough to keep me in sight but giving us space.

"Ollie," I whisper, nodding toward the approaching guards. "Your men are coming."

He pulls back just enough to peer down the corridor.

A plate crashes in a nearby room. I seize the moment, grabbing his wrist and pulling him through a pair of swinging doors into a massive kitchen. The room buzzes with activity—head chef barking orders, waitstaff hustling in and out, balancing elegant dishes.

"Miss Hastings?"

An assistant cook looks up from chopping vegetables, her eyes widening when she spots Ollie behind me. She drops her knife in surprise and oddly bows. It's not every day that Prince Oliver, heir to the British throne, and the First Daughter of the United States crash through your kitchen.

"Uh," Ollie scans the room, panic rising in his eyes. "Is there a back door out of here?"

We're running out of time before security catches up, especially after our less-than-subtle detour into the kitchen.

"Just need some fresh air," Ollie says, tugging at his collar like he's struggling to breathe.

The assistant cook points toward a door at the far end of the kitchen. We weave quickly toward it, ignoring the whispers and curious stares trailing us.

We reach the back door just as it swings open, slamming into me. I stumble backward into Ollie, who catches me before I fall.

A guy about our age, dressed like waitstaff, looks up in surprise as he pockets a phone in his back pocket. He opens his mouth—probably to call out who we are, as if we don't already know—when security appears at the other end of the kitchen. Instinct kicks in, and I shove him back through the door into a narrow alley.

There's something about him that doesn't scream stranger danger or, more importantly, murderer vibes. He seems like an innocent caught up in our escape plan by bad luck. If Ollie and I end up the subject of a true crime podcast, I'll die embarrassed that my instincts were so off.

"Do you have a car?" Ollie asks.

"Just my skateboard," he says, and the trapped feeling tightens around me.

I poke my head out from the alley onto the street. A large crowd of press and spectators has gathered, blocking the way. I duck back into the shadows, moving quickly toward Ollie and the waiter.

"The street's a no-go."

At least we made it out of the building this time — more than I managed on my last try, when I didn't even reach the end of the hall.

Ollie hurries to a parked catering van and peers in through the window. He turns to me with a grin. "Keys are in the ignition. Let's go!" He swings open the passenger door and jumps inside.

"Um," the waiter says as Ollie leans out the window.

"Hurry up!" Ollie motions at me, "You drive, speed demon."

"I can't let you take that." The guy watches us like we're some kind of prank gone rogue.

"Sorry, it's a matter of national security," I say, already running toward the driver's side.

"Callie's Catering van?"

I don't answer, opening the door and about to climb in, when he gently grabs my arm, stopping me.

"I could get fired for this."

"We'll replace the company's van with a dozen new ones, okay? We have to go. Now!"

Ollie reaches over the seats, pulling me inside the van as the back door slides open and security pours out.

"I'll drive," the guy says quickly. I jump in and slide into the middle seat while he hops in and puts the van in drive, just as a guard reaches Ollie's door.

We peel out onto the street. Ollie and I both slouch down in our seats, hiding behind the dashboard line from the crowd gathered outside the main doors. They're hoping for a glimpse of any esteemed guests at tonight's event, unaware that two high-profile attendees are currently fleeing the scene in the catering van.

"Hey, so," the guy's voice is surprisingly calm for someone aiding fugitives—okay, not technically fugitives, but it sure feels like it right now. "They're chasing us."

I poke my head up and glance in his side mirror. A few security guards are chasing us on foot. I lean toward the steering wheel, pressing my palm firmly on the horn to clear the way as the driver weaves the van through traffic and indifferent pedestrians blocking the road.

"Make a turn somewhere, we need to get off this main road. It's basically gridlock!" Ollie says, sitting up and buckling his seatbelt. The driver obeys, managing to slip off the main road and ditch the security on foot.

"We need to get as far away from here as possible." I keep my eyes glued to the side mirrors, waiting for sirens and flashing lights to close in. "They'll regroup fast and be on us in no time.”

The driver shoots me a wide-eyed glance, flicking his gaze between Ollie and me. “Am I harboring fugitives?” He glances in the rearview mirror, then back at us. “Did you steal the Declaration of Independence or something?”

I bite my bottom lip, stealing a glance at Ollie. “Nothing like that, don’t worry.”

Before he can say more, sirens wail in the distance. I twist in my seat, trying to pinpoint their location as the driver noticeably picks up speed.

“This doesn’t feel like nothing.”

“Just don’t stop. Please.” I plead. Thankfully, he doesn’t.

We drive for twenty minutes, taking rights and lefts at random to avoid any straight route. Eventually, the boy pulls into an underground parking lot and drives down to the nearly empty bottom floor before parking the van.

“I’m so fired.”

“Sorry,” I mutter, as Ollie rests his head against the back of the seat.

“Possibly going to jail too?”

“No,” I say, just as Ollie replies, “Probably.”

I shoot Ollie a look before turning back to the boy and putting on my fake megawatt smile — the one I save for the press. “What’s your name?”

“Noah?”

I laugh, and the smile turns genuine. “Why do you

sound unsure? That's really your name, isn't it?"

"It is. I just wasn't expecting the question. Also, not sure I should've told you that."

"I have connections, so if you do get arrested, I'll handle it. What's your last name?"

"Connections? That sounds ominous."

"Just trust her, mate—she knows the President of your country," Ollie adds as he opens the glovebox, rifling through the papers inside. No clue what he's looking for, if anything.

"You do?" He eyes me skeptically. I give a small nod.

"Uh, yeah. So what's your last name, just in case? I need to know who to ask for." I'm not sure how much influence I really have, but he doesn't need to know that. I'll make sure they don't charge him with anything insane, like kidnapping or whatever else they might try.

"It's Hart. Do I get your names?"

"It's best if you don't."

Noah studies me carefully, like he's trying to figure out the type of people he just helped escape. Meanwhile, I'm sizing him up for a different reason—he's cute. Really cute. Fitted white shirt, black slacks, black apron still tied around his waist. Scuffed Nikes make me smile. Murderer? Could be. Cute guys can be murderers, right? Ted Bundy definitely had fans writing him letters while behind bars.

That thought nudges me closer to Ollie, though the van's middle seat barely leaves room to move.

I try to look at him without making it obvious, but I'm distracted by the thought that his idea of fleeing security might lead us straight to a murder house. Would I even recognize a murder house if we pulled up to one? Actually, do murder houses even exist? Maybe he's taking us to an abandoned warehouse.

"What?" Noah asks, catching my analyzing gaze. My eyes snap back to his dark brown ones.

"Nothing, I just, um," I break our eye contact, feeling my skin flush. "I like your shoes."

Noah looks surprised, then confused at what I've said. Before he can respond, Ollie slams the glovebox shut, making me jump.

I turn to him, grateful for the distraction as he twists in his seat to look behind us into the van.

"You don't happen to have any food still back there, do you?"

"No, sorry, man," Noah says, but glances toward the back anyway. He scratches the back of his neck and looks between Ollie and me. "I only live a few miles from here. We can grab something and eat it there, if you want."

"Please!" Ollie says excitedly, his voice louder than my quiet "no thanks."

Both boys hear me, turning toward me. "We don't want to impose," I say lightly, hoping not to offend. He may be cute and helped us escape the gala, but that doesn't mean we're about to go to his house. What if he says one thing but really takes us to some abandoned place to kill us or hold us for ransom? Or... ugh. These thoughts aren't mine—they're my dad's and the security team's. They should be mine since it's reckless and stupid, but I'm starving, and the clock's already ticking down on my freedom.

Ollie sees it on my face before I say anything and grins. "Please, can we get Taco Bell?"

CHAPTER 2

Before we leave the parking garage in search of something edible, Noah jumps out of the van to call his roommates. He wants to make sure the coast is clear, no unexpected guests hanging around. I'm still not sure if he knows exactly who we are, but he mutters something about not needing witnesses to the crime of "aiding and abetting fugitives" before walking off with his phone pressed to his ear.

He doesn't go far, just enough to be out of earshot, but still visible through the windshield.

"El?" Ollie's voice pulls me away from watching Noah pace. I turn toward him.

"I'm really sorry about that whole neck-kissing act back at the gala. It was a weird move. I figured some awkward PDA might make people uncomfortable enough to look away. Buy us a little space."

I laugh, quick and loud. "And here I thought you had a thing for necks. Can you imagine the headlines if the press caught that? Prince Gets Intimate in Gala Escape."

Ollie shakes his head, his smile small but real.

The truth is, despite what the tabloids think, Ollie and I

aren't romantically involved. We never were. Never will be. Our worlds collided by coincidence, and somehow, without warning, he became my best friend.

"We did it. We actually did it."

Ollie spins in a slow circle, eyes scanning the empty road like he can't quite believe we're alone.

"Nobody's watching our every move."

He slings an arm around my shoulders, pulling me in like we just robbed a bank and got away with it.

"We're actually free, Els."

I lean my head on his shoulder.

"We're going to be in so much trouble."

"You more than me, though."

"Why?" he asks.

"Because I'm just the First Daughter. You're a future king."

The thing is, this isn't our first escape attempt. We've tried badly and failed more than a few times.

I'm not saying we don't have good lives. We do. We're privileged, no question. We've traveled the world, attended royal galas, and been backstage at concerts most people would kill to see.

But I'm twenty-two. And as much as I love Taylor Swift, that whole "miserable and magical" vibe? Yeah, heavy on the miserable. It's not so magical when your idea of rebellion is slipping past the palace gates without a security alert.

While everyone else my age is off eating midnight waffles in some sketchy diner with their friends, I've got a dozen agents in black suits tracking my heartbeat like I'm a national asset.

Most twenty-somethings are knee-deep in college life—if they haven't already graduated. Their weeknights are fueled by late-night study sessions, their weekends packed with football games and overcrowded house parties. It's the classic coming-of-age experience, complete with caffeine and regret.

People often ask why I've never enrolled in college.

The truth? While everyone else was researching schools and stressing over personal statements, I was crisscrossing the country on my dad's presidential campaign trail. After that, I was catapulted into the role of First Daughter, and somewhere along the way, I lost myself in that persona.

It doesn't help that everyone around me—especially Dad—has a blueprint for my future. They think I should pursue something important, like Political Science. Or better yet, follow my golden-boy older brother Grant to law school.

Honestly, it all sounds mind-numbingly dull. Maybe that's part of why I keep putting off college. I can't imagine myself buried in politics for the rest of my life.

So, for now, my weeknights and weekends blur together into the same monotonous loop:

Home.

Usually curled up on the couch, watching some

cringey, addictive reality show.

Meanwhile, the rest of the house hums with activity well into the night.

Dad's in his office, locked in meetings with world leaders across time zones, combing through legislation, prepping speeches—doing whatever presidents do.

Secret Service agents line the hallways, stationed day and night. I can't even sneak to the kitchen for a midnight snack without being shadowed.

Technically, I'm never alone.

But I've never felt lonelier.

I see people constantly chasing virality, desperate for a sliver of spotlight.

Me? I'd give anything just to disappear into a crowd. To walk into a store alone—truly alone—not shadowed by someone "giving me space" while trailing a few feet behind.

I still think about the university visit during one of Dad's speaking gigs. While he met with the president and a circle of local leaders, a campus guide took Mom and me on a tour.

I was nineteen, surrounded by hundreds of students my age, all hurrying to and from classes. Some sat in loose study huddles outside classrooms, and others stopped to chat with friends they bumped into.

And me? I couldn't stop smiling.

We visited the library, the planetarium, the student

center, and even the football stadium. But it wasn't the buildings that stayed with me. It was the feeling.

Freedom.

Normalcy.

I wanted that.

To belong somewhere.

To blend in. Just another student with earbuds in and coffee in hand.

And for a moment, I loved it. Every second of it.

Until I didn't.

Because, of course, we had a team trailing us. Secret Service in their grim suits, standing out like bruises against the backdrop of ripped jeans and oversized sweatshirts. The campus was on high alert the whole time, and though I was used to it, it still stung.

But the worst part wasn't the visibility.

It happened in a hallway in the business building.

A boy walking toward us swung his backpack around to his chest and started unzipping it.

His eyes met mine.

And in that split second, I knew.

Something was about to go very, very wrong.

He reached into his bag.

In an instant, one of Mom's agents slammed him to the ground, pinning his arm behind his back with a knee to his spine.

The others moved fast, surrounding Mom and me, pushing us into a stairwell so aggressively it felt like we were under siege.

"It's just a calculator!" he shouted, voice cracking with panic.

A calculator.

Just a boy on his way to class, reaching for his calculator—and taken down like a criminal.

I understood. I still do. Their job is to protect us. But understanding didn't stop the guilt from slicing through me like glass.

The kid was humiliated. And by now, someone in the crowd had definitely recorded it. The video would hit the internet within the hour.

For the people who already hate everything my dad stands for, this would be fuel. They'd twist it, spin it, and blow it up into something worse—and it was already bad.

Ollie would get it. He always does.

My best friend has lived under surveillance since birth. Heir to the British crown. Watched, whispered about, tracked by tabloids that never sleep.

He's so tired.

He just wants a real vacation. Not the kind where headlines erupt because he dared to relax on a beach while the world kept spinning in crisis mode. A proper break, where he's not flanked by a security detail every five feet.

That's why Ollie and I stage these little escape attempts. We don't want much—just a moment to be ourselves. Truly ourselves.

The farthest we've ever made it was during a formal event at Buckingham Palace. We slipped away and reached Clarence House—his family's residence—before security shut us down.

And it wasn't even suspicious. We just wanted to walk through London like normal people. Pretend, for one night, that we weren't who we are. But one of the guards in the tunnel between the palace and Clarence House snitched. For all they knew, we were just going to his place to ditch the party. That was the idea, anyway.

We had even changed into casual clothes. Hoodies, sneakers, the whole off-duty royal act. But the moment we stepped out the front door of Clarence House, they were already waiting.

I get it. With our track record, security's basically programmed to go on high alert the second we're in the same room. Which is why I'm honestly stunned we successfully made it out the door and practically to the street.

Sure, we barely made it. If this van hadn't been sitting out back with the keys basically screaming 'steal me', we'd still be cornered in that alley.

But the important point is—we made it.

We're out.

And yes, maybe we just hitched a ride with someone who could be a budding criminal mastermind, but right now? I'm holding tight to the fleeting joy of Taylor Swift crooning, "happy, free, confused, and lonely at the same time."

Because, for once, I actually get it.

The driver's side door swings open, and I jolt upright from where I'd been slouched against Ollie.

"Sorry to interrupt," Noah says, buckling in. "Let's go get some food."

CHAPTER 3

Noah had asked his roommates, Sawyer and Leah, to grab us Taco Bell so we wouldn't have to drive the catering van—a rolling billboard to security and law enforcement that practically screams our location.

Just like Noah said, his house isn't far from the parking garage. But the moment I spot a car with its headlights on parked right outside, my heart jumps into my throat. Instinctively, I grab Ollie's arm. Busted.

Noah notices as he pulls the van into the narrow driveway. "Don't worry," he says quickly, "that's just my roommate. She's moving her car so we can park farther up the driveway, away from the street."

I can't help but wonder how that conversation went: "Hey, can you move your car so I can hide a catering van in the driveway?" I don't ask, though. I'm too busy watching as he pulls up as far as he can, then shifts the van into park. The car waiting in front of the house slowly rolls in behind us.

Noah hops out to talk to his roommate, and I glance at Ollie. He looks completely unfazed, like we didn't just ditch our Secret Service detail and end up at some guy's house. But he knows I'm spiraling because he reaches over and gives my hand a reassuring squeeze.

"Come on, Els," he says with a grin, "I'm starving. It's going to be fine."

We step into the house through the side door by the driveway, leading straight into the kitchen. Ollie wastes no time, settling at the table where a couple of Taco Bell bags wait. I follow, but take in my surroundings instead of the food.

It's quaint. The brick walls and old-fashioned kitchen add a certain charm. The house is clean and smells faintly of fresh lemon. Did one of Noah's roommates scrub the place knowing we'd come, or is it always this tidy? A small pile of mail sits on the counter—I glance at it, relaxing just a little when I see it's addressed to Noah Hart. Good, he's not lying about his name.

Noah enters the kitchen through the side door, followed by a petite blonde with shoulder-length hair. "Hi, I'm Leah."

"Hi." I don't offer our names, and she doesn't ask. Still, she looks confused by my silence. I watch her carefully as I sit at the table, searching for any sign of recognition or betrayal, like she's already tipped off the authorities to our location. Noah takes a seat beside me, but my eyes stay fixed on Leah, who tries not to openly assess Ollie.

My stomach drops—and not the fun rollercoaster kind. Does she recognize him after all? Her gaze flicks back to me, and I'm almost certain she knows who we are. This could be bad. Our brief taste of freedom might come crashing down because of some Kristen Bell lookalike.

The doorbell rings, and we all freeze. Ollie literally pauses, taco halfway to his mouth. This is it. Kristen Bell didn't even have to rat us out—security tracked us before she got the chance. Of course they did. They found out who Noah was through Callie's Catering and got his home address, or maybe tracked his phone. Either way, we're doomed, and I didn't even get to enjoy an insanely unhealthy Taco Bell burrito.

Leah lets out a slight laugh, breaking our frozen stances. "Are you guys okay? You look like you've seen a ghost. That's just my boyfriend, Max."

She stands and places her hands on Noah's shoulders, squeezing as she passes him. "See you later. Tomorrow probably." She grabs a small crossbody bag tossed half-hazardly on the side table. "Bye, Noah's friends."

"Thanks for the tacos!" Ollie calls after her, returning to his food. I, however, remain alert—still unsure if it's actually her boyfriend at the door.

I strain to hear as she opens it, having convinced myself I'd recognize the voice on the other side. The door closes, and no rush of security comes trampling through the house. I lean back in my chair with a quiet sigh, allowing myself to relax.

"Eat, Els." Ollie slides a paper-wrapped taco across the table to me.

I unwrap it slowly, my stomach doing a weird flip, not from hunger, but nerves.

"So…" Noah leans forward, tone casual, but there's a

flicker of curiosity in his eyes. "Can I ask what your next plan of action is?"

The question is aimed at me, but he flicks a glance toward Ollie, who's currently inhaling his taco like he hasn't eaten in days. I know Ollie's been taught proper table etiquette, but I guess that doesn't count when it comes to Taco Bell?

"Honestly?" I shrug, taking a bite mostly to avoid answering right away. "They'll be here any minute, especially once they get your info from Callie's Catering. I'm half surprised they haven't tracked us down already after the parking garage."

"And 'they' being… who exactly?" Noah's voice is light, but his gaze sharpens.

Ollie chimes in, unhelpfully, "The Secret Service."

I shoot him a sharp look. He keeps chewing, like he didn't just drop a huge, stressful bomb on Noah's lap. Noah nods slowly, like he suspected as much.

"It might take them longer than you think," he says. "Callie's Catering doesn't actually have me in their system."

I stiffen—red flags, sirens, danger music playing in my head. He's going to kidnap us. He's part of something bigger. Was this Taco Bell drugged? I feel dizzy. Is my tongue going numb? This was all a trap—

"I went in place of my friend," Noah interrupts my spiraling thoughts, his voice calm. "I pretended to be him."

I sit up straight, eyes narrowing. "You don't actually work for Callie's Catering?"

He shakes his head. "Nope. My friend Nate does. His girlfriend surprised him by flying in last-minute, so he asked me to cover for him. It's his second job—he's trying to pay off some debts and save for an engagement ring. So, I filled in." He pauses, grimacing slightly. "He's not going to be thrilled I got him fired, though."

"That's fantastic news," Ollie says brightly, sipping his drink. "I mean, not for your friend but now we just have to wait for them to track your phone." He says it like it's the most casual thing.

"You two really don't do much to ease my suspicions that I'm harboring two on-the-run fugitives," Noah mutters, a smirk tugging at his mouth.

"On the run? Yes," Ollie replies, unfazed. "Fugitives? Not exactly."

CHAPTER 4

After we eat, we drift into Noah's living room. I perch on the edge of the couch, careful not to sink in too far or give myself permission to relax. It's too soon for that.

The room is mostly bare, but a few details confirm it's lived in, not just some lifeless Airbnb. A PlayStation lies beneath the wall-mounted TV, surrounded by scattered game cases. A self-help book sits half-forgotten on a side table, its pages slightly curled. Above the couch, a framed jersey hangs like a personal trophy.

Ollie shrugs off his tux jacket and loosens his tie before dropping beside me, unbothered and sprawling like this is normal. How someone constantly in the spotlight isn't more cautious of strangers is beyond me. But I guess that's just Ollie.

Noah starts toward the accent chair in the corner but pauses when the side door opens and his other roommate, Sawyer, walks in.

They greet each other with casual familiarity. I stay quiet, tuning into their conversation from the couch.

Thankfully, Noah doesn't mention how Ollie and I turned up on his doorstep like a royal scandal waiting to happen.

Surprisingly, and thankfully, Sawyer doesn't comment on our black-tie attire. We're introduced to him in the same awkward way we met Leah, without even sharing our names.

As he and Ollie chat, Ollie spins some story about living somewhere in London — which is technically true. I can't stop watching Noah though as Ollie talks. He watches us the way someone studies a puzzle, trying to figure out where all the strange pieces go. And, to be fair, we are exactly that.

Sawyer, who I've learned works in IT, glances from Noah to me.

"You guys staying?" he asks.

I look over at Ollie. He's curled into the corner of the couch, eyes closed, completely checked out.

"Yes," Noah answers before I can. I turn my attention back to him.

"I mean, we don't have a guest room," he adds, "but we can make up some beds on the floor in here."

I have no idea where else we'd go. And honestly, by tomorrow we'll be back to our regularly scheduled lives. So why not? Sleep on the floor at our getaway driver's house — sounds about right.

Sawyer steps out to grab extra blankets for our makeshift beds so Ollie can sleep. Noah disappears down the hall and returns with spare clothes for both Ollie and me. I'm more grateful than I can say to finally shed the dress.

I excuse myself to change in the bathroom. Noah has given me a loose pair of black joggers and a soft, plain white T-shirt. Without thinking, I lift the shirt to my nose and inhale. It smells like him—woodsy, like cedar and pine. The realization makes my cheeks burn, and I quickly drop my hand.

When I return to the living room, Ollie is already curled into the blankets on the floor. He's changed into red-and-blue plaid pajama bottoms and a faded graphic tee. The whole scene feels strangely... childlike. I smile, unable to help it. Knowing Ollie's background, I doubt he's ever slept on a floor in his life.

"You should take my bed," Noah says, nodding toward the hallway. "I'll sleep out here on the couch."

"No, I can't take your bed. I'm fine out here, but thank you."

I cross the room and settle beside him.

Noah looks at me for a moment like he's about to say something, but instead, he leans over and switches off the lamp beside the couch. The room dims, lit only by the soft glow from the microwave light in the nearby kitchen.

"I'd better let you get some sleep. I don't need to worry about you two robbing us blind, do I?"

There's a slight curve to his mouth—enough to tell he's joking, though a sliver of truth might still be tucked behind the smile. Letting two 'fugitives' crash in your living room after helping them flee a high-society gala isn't exactly sane.

"Good night," he says, pushing himself off the couch.

"Ellie," I whisper into the darkness before I can stop myself.

"What?" Noah whispers back.

"My name. It's Ellie."

He pauses, then sinks back onto the couch.

"Do you have a last name, Ellie?"

I study his face in the shadows. He's definitely attractive. His hair, once perfectly styled, now sticks up in wild directions from all the times he's run his fingers through it tonight. A small scar near his left eyebrow catches my eye, and I have to grip the blanket just to keep from reaching out and touching it.

"No last name then? Iconic enough to go by one, like Cher or Zendaya?"

I laugh, the sound light but real.

He tilts his head toward the floor where Ollie is sleeping. "Does your boyfriend have a last name? Or a first one?"

"He's not my boyfriend." I glance down at Ollie, watching the slow rise and fall of his chest. I don't know why I need him to understand that Ollie and I aren't a thing, but I do.

"He actually has several last names. I can barely remember them all. First name's Ollie—well, Oliver— but I call him Ollie."

"So, not a boyfriend, you're just in business together," Noah says, raising an eyebrow. "You know, the business of stealing the Declaration of Independence—or whatever it is you two do. Tell me, what does a Brit want with it? Planning to take it back to the King and reclaim the colonies?"

"Oh shoot, you figured out our plan," I reply deadpan. "Except, England has a Queen now, so we're actually taking it to her."

I laugh as his eyes widen in mock alarm. Holding up my pinky, I grin. "I promise you, not only did we not steal the Declaration of Independence, we didn't steal anything."

Noah hooks his pinky with mine, playing along—and there it is. A small flutter in my stomach.

Ridiculous. A pinky promise? Am I really so starved for normal interaction that a simple touch sets me off?

I pull my hand back a second too quickly, trying to brush it off. "Well, I guess… aside from the van. But don't worry, we're just borrowing that."

Noah doesn't answer right away. I can feel his eyes on me, and for a moment, the only sound in the night is Ollie's slow, even breathing.

"Thanks again for everything today," I say, my voice quieter now. "We owe you more than you'll ever know."

Noah leans forward, resting his elbows on his knees. "Hey, it was either definitely get fired helping my friend or… get fired and return the van. At least this way, I get a story out of it."

I let out a quiet laugh. "Right. Do it for the plot."

"Do it for the plot," he echoes with a grin as he stands. "I'll let you get some sleep. Sweet dreams, Ellie."

There's something about the way he says my name—soft, careful, like he means it—that sends a ripple through my chest. The small flutters in my stomach multiply, fast and warm.

CHAPTER 5

The next morning, I woke to find Ollie already gone. For a brief moment, panic rises—until his laugh echoes from the kitchen, followed by the soft click of a closing door. I follow the sounds and spot Ollie sitting alone at the small kitchen table.

"Good morning," I yawn, fingers attempting to tame my wild bed hair.

"Morning, sunshine. What's the plan for today? We're not just heading back, right?" Ollie asks, pouring a bowl of Lucky Charms. I doubt he's ever had them before now.

"No," I say, grabbing a box of Cinnamon Toast Crunch and a bowl. Someone's laid out a buffet of sugary cereals and navy blue bowls with matching spoons. "But we can't really go anywhere without being spotted. So much for freedom when you still can't leave the house."

Noah and Sawyer come in from the outside. Sawyer gives me a quick nod before switching on the TV in the living room. Noah takes the seat beside me.

"Good morning. Did you sleep okay?"

"For sleeping in a stranger's house, I slept pretty well."

"We need to get out of the city," Ollie says, still focused on our conversation. "Mate, is there a train station nearby?"

"Are you kidding? You know, public transport hubs are heavily guarded." I point out.

"What are you guys talking about?" Noah pours himself a bowl of Cinnamon Toast Crunch.

Neither Ollie nor I answers as I turn back to him. "Maybe we could Uber to Baltimore, then go from there. Outside DC should be less watched."

I glance at Noah. "Think one of your roommates would let us use their Uber account? I'd ask you, but they probably have your details already—and might be looking you up."

"You know, saying things like that doesn't exactly ease my anxiety from yesterday's events."

Leah steps into the kitchen and takes a seat at the table, cutting me off before I can say more about our next move. She was already watching us yesterday—if she hasn't put the pieces together yet, it's only a matter of time.

After switching on the TV, Sawyer joins us at the table.

"Last night, the Queen of England and her children, Prince Oliver and Princess Sophie, attended the First Lady's fundraiser gala, where the First Lady was accompanied by her husband, President Hastings, and their daughter, Eleanor," a voice echoes from the living room.

Ollie and I snap our attention to the screen, where

images of his family—and then mine—flash by, entering the event. Worse, we're photographed wearing the same clothes we left folded in the living room.

The channel flips to a sitcom. I glance at Noah as he sets the remote down on the table.

"The news is boring," he explains, shoveling another spoonful of cereal into his mouth. Sawyer and Leah exchange a brief glance before turning their attention back to Ollie and me.

"Um," I glance at Ollie, then back to Leah and Sawyer, "would either of you mind if we ordered an Uber using your accounts?"

"No need, I'll drive you," Noah replies quickly.

"What?" Ollie and I exchange a look, then turn back to Noah.

"I'll drive."

"You don't even know where we're going."

"Okay," he leans back in his chair. "Where are you headed?"

"It doesn't matter," I say, as Ollie adds, "Baltimore."

I shoot him a look. He shrugs, shoveling a spoonful of Lucky Charms into his mouth.

"What's in Baltimore?" Leah asks, and I wish I had a clear answer. I can't exactly say it's simply to avoid the watchful eyes we have in DC.

"What's not in Baltimore is the better question," Ollie replies, pouring more cereal into his bowl.

"Right, okay," Leah replies, clearly not buying our excitement about Baltimore, "Does your amazing trip include a stop at a clothing store, or are you planning to wear that fancy dress?"

I hadn't even thought about what to wear. Leah must have read my mind because she smiles and stands up from the table.

"Come on, I've got something you can wear."

Twenty minutes later, after a quick de-makeover courtesy of Leah, I head back into the kitchen where Ollie and Noah are sitting alone, talking about some superhero movie.

I'm wearing faded jeans and a gray Washington DC crewneck that Leah lent me. The pins and curls from last night are now loose waves, and Leah insisted on just mascara and lip gloss to let my 'natural beauty' show through.

But the way Noah's eyes sweep over me, you'd think I was still in that expensive dress from last night.

"Oh, Els!" Ollie exclaims when he spots me. "What if we do a road trip? Noah can drive us."

Noah turns to me with a smile, like the idea is perfect, but I shake my head, dampening their excitement.

"No, sorry. I appreciate you helping us last night, I really do. But no offense, I'm not about to go on a road trip with a stranger."

"I'm not strange, I'm Noah." He places an open palm on his chest, then raises both hands in the air. "Okay, okay.

Let's see." His eyes narrow in concentration before returning to me. "Hate tomatoes. Love ketchup. My favorite era is Red." He smirks at the confused look on my face. "Taylor Swift, keep up. Oh! And I can divide any number by 17. Go on, quiz me."

I cross my arms on the table and lean forward. "2,362."

"43."

I roll my eyes, turning to Ollie, who looks impressed. "Wow, you did that so quickly in your head."

"I'm fairly sure you're nowhere near right, but I don't have a way to check."

"Kind of like you don't know if you can trust me? I did help you steal the Declaration of Independence, didn't I?"

"Whoa, what?" Sawyer strolls into the kitchen, eyes wide and frantic as he takes in all of us.

"Relax, it's an inside joke." Noah winks at me — a look I wish I could rewind and replay in my memory, over and over.

"See? We've already got an inside joke. I'm definitely no stranger."

"Come on, Els. Let's do it. What better taste of freedom than the open road? Besides, we could use a driver."

"Hey, I drive!" I shoot Ollie an appalled look.

"When was the last time you actually got behind the wheel?" He doesn't wait for an answer before turning to Noah. "You're in."

"Wait." I watch Noah and Ollie shake hands like they

just closed a business deal. "What's in it for you? Why would you want to gallivant with two fugitives?"

"I thought you two weren't fugitives?" Noah smiles, clearly enjoying the jab. "Besides, this comes at perfect timing. My boss is making me take PTO next week—I've maxed out my hours, and we both know Callie's Catering isn't going to call anytime soon to have me cover for my friend. Plus, I've always wanted to go on a road trip. Movies make it look fun."

I say nothing, staring down at the table as I think. It's not that I don't trust Noah—he's been nothing but kind, and he doesn't give off any creepy vibes—but I can only imagine what my dad and my nice little security entourage would say, knowing I've not only run off with this boy from the gala but am now planning a road trip with him.

"Come on, Els, we wanted an adventure. He can help us have it!"

That's how fifteen minutes later, we're on the road in Leah's car. She and Sawyer promised to return the catering van to wherever Callie's Catering is based. Taking Noah's car wasn't an option—knowing they're probably already looking for it—and he had to leave his phone behind, too. After a quick stop at a nearby ATM so Noah and I could each withdraw some cash and avoid being tracked, we finally hit the road.

No phones, limited cash, and a prayer that we actually make it out of the city.

CHAPTER 6

So, city of dreams? Baltimore?" Noah asks, teasing me, knowing full well we don't have a real plan.

"That was before the road trip. Not much of a road trip if we just go to Baltimore," Ollie says, leaning forward and poking his head between the front seats.

"Good, because technically, I'm headed toward Pennsylvania, not Baltimore."

"So, where then?" Ollie asks. "Should we just drive and see where we end up?"

"Where would you go if you could go anywhere?" I ask Noah. I've been to plenty of places across the country, but there's nowhere I'm desperate to visit. This trip is about the journey, not the destination.

Noah pauses briefly.

"Southern California."

"Why? The beach?" I turn slightly in my seat to face him better.

Noah shakes his head but keeps his eyes on the road.

"My grandma lives in Irvine. I don't really know her—she's my mom's mom." He swallows, searching for the right words. "My mom left when I was five. Grandma tried to keep in touch with Dad and me, still unhappy with Mom's decision to leave and act like she didn't have a family. Dad and I moved around a lot when I was younger, and eventually, between the moves and the distance, we just lost contact. She's the only family I've really got left."

I don't know what to say. Sorry feels too small, and I can tell Noah doesn't want my sympathy or for the conversation to head further into his family history. It's a heavy topic with someone you barely know.

"Okay," I say, "California it is. I've always wanted to go to Disneyland. What do you think, Ollie?"

"I like it as long as I can touch the Pacific Ocean."

"No way, high demands there, man." Noah teases, and Ollie laughs.

"Right? I'm really just here to escape being watched at every turn. To experience the land and the people who revolted against my ancestors."

Noah glances in the rearview mirror at Ollie. I watch him carefully, searching for any sign of recognition, but his face remains unreadable.

I sigh and lean back in the chair, keeping my eyes on Noah. "You know, don't you?"

His gaze flicks briefly to mine. "Know what?"

"Who we are."

He rubs the back of his neck. "Yeah, I was working the event. Half the kitchen staff wouldn't stop talking about how 'dreamy' Prince Oliver is. Their words, not mine." Noah shifts his eyes back to Ollie in the mirror.

"They said I'm dreamy? Awe, that's cute."

"Why didn't you say anything?"

He shrugs. "Pretty obvious you didn't want me to know."

"And you're okay with this? Taking two fairly high-profile people across the country?" I raise an eyebrow.

He shrugs again, glancing at me briefly before returning his focus to the road. "Can't say I love the idea of you two sneaking around, but hey, now I get to visit my grandma. Besides, a bit of teenage rebellion never hurt anyone."

"You do know we're not teenagers, right?" Ollie pops his head up.

"Close enough. With the life you've led, you're like twelve and sixty rolled into one."

Ollie leans in towards me, stage-whispering, "I don't think that's a compliment."

After driving for a few hours, we pull off the freeway into a small town stuck in the middle of nowhere to gas up. I'm not too worried about being seen here, but the place barely qualifies as a town — just farmland with scattered houses, small and bare.

Once Noah fills the tank, Ollie watches eagerly, as if watching someone fill a car is the most exciting thing he's experienced. Noah runs inside to use the bathroom as Ollie and I stretch by the car before climbing back in. We watch as Noah exits the station. Instead of returning to the driver's seat, he walks straight over and opens the passenger door. I freeze, halfway through buckling up, and look at him, confused.

"Do you want me to drive?"

"No, not that." He shakes his head and hands me a small black phone. "It's a burner — can't be traced. Your parents won't know where you are, but they need to know you're safe."

I stare at the phone in his outstretched hand, as if it might explode any moment. I glance back at Noah, who nods encouragingly.

"If my dad were still around, I know he'd be beside himself if I disappeared," he adds—and I know he's right.

With a small sigh, I take the phone and climb out of the car, heading toward a patch of grass beside the gas station. Thankfully, I have Maggie—my dad's chief of staff—number memorized. A true talent in this modern age. I dial, and after a few rings, she picks up.

"Hey Mags," I say hesitantly. Not just anyone has her number, so thankfully, she answers my unknown caller ID.

"Ellie!" Her voice is immediate, sharp with concern. "Where are you? Are you safe? Are you okay?"

"I'm fine. I promise. Is Dad busy? Can I talk with him?"

She's silent for a moment—I imagine her walking into my dad's office, telling him it's me before transferring the call. The phone barely rings before he picks up.

"Eleanor?"

I close my eyes at the sound of his voice. He sounds worried, angry.

"Hi Dad."

I hear his sigh of relief. "Where are you? Sweetheart, we'll have some guys to you in no time."

"Ollie and I are fine, really. We just need some freedom, Dad."

"Freedom? Eleanor, he's the future King of England, and you're the first daughter of this country. It's incredibly dangerous for you two to be gallivanting about alone. You've had your fun—now come home."

"No."

"Eleanor, now." Not a suggestion, an order.

"I'm not a kid, Dad. Ollie and I want an adventure, okay? We'll come home after."

"An adventure? You've had plenty of those under the Secret Service's care."

"That's not the same, and you know it." I'm stubborn, refusing to crack.

"El—"

"I gotta go, Dad. I love you. Tell Mom hi!" I hang up before he can say more.

I turn back toward the car, where Noah leans against it, watching me closely. His arms are crossed over his chest, looking like he belongs on the cover of a magazine rather than at a gas station in Pennsylvania. The backseat window is rolled down, and Ollie rests his folded arms on the open windowsill.

"That sounded like it went as expected?" Ollie asks, giving me a slightly pitying look, like he knows exactly what kind of conversation took place.

I pull a face, then reach out the phone to Ollie. "Yup, now it's your turn."

"I'm going to be beheaded for this, aren't I?" Noah says as we watch Ollie get out of the car.

"Nah, they stopped beheading ages ago. Maybe tossed in a dungeon, though."

"You think you're so funny," Noah bumps his hip into mine. I turn to him with a grin.

"Yeah, I actually do."

CHAPTER 7

We finally stopped for the night in Pittsburgh. We drive until we find the first run-down motel that won't ask for ID to check in. No chances taken.

Ollie pokes his head between our seats as we eye the place. The neon "No Vacancy" sign flickers and has the letter T missing entirely from the blocked 'motel' letters.

"No time like the present to catch bed bugs—or whatever disease has infested this dump," Ollie says, shivering dramatically like the thought's crawling under his skin.

"Close your eyes and pretend it's the Ritz-Carlton," I tease, even though I'm just as sure we're leaving with some kind of infection. "I'm pretty sure every horror movie ever was filmed here," I whisper, making Noah and Ollie chuckle.

"Hey, we could go somewhere nicer."

"No," I shake my head, glancing from Noah back out at the motel. "Not unless you have a fake ID." I pause, eyes on him. "*Do* you have a fake ID?"

Ollie and I exchange hopeful looks, but Noah turns off the car. "Looks like we're staying here."

To save money, we book just one room with two queen beds. It's not as bad as I expected. I'm not sure if I thought there'd be stained sheets or blood dripping from the vents, but instead there's ugly mustard-yellow paisley wallpaper and a faint musty smell.

I go straight to the window, hoping for a decent view, only to find a cement wall so close I could open the window and touch it. I laugh, then close the curtains. Honestly, I'm not sure why the curtains are even there. They don't offer any privacy, and the wall blocks out all the sunlight anyway.

Ollie jumps onto one of the beds, his eyes fixed on the wallpaper. "I'd love to have a conversation with whoever picked this design. What made them think this was the best choice? Were the other options any better?"

Noah chuckles, grabbing the remote and flicking on the small TV.

"I'm surprised your faces aren't plastered all over the news by now." Noah flips from CNN to Fox News, then to a local station, before settling on *The Big Bang Theory*.

"That'd cause way too many security headaches," Ollie says, propping himself up on his elbows and half-watching Sheldon and Penny argue on screen.

"I'm going to get some ice." I reach for the small black ice bucket on the table beside the TV, already half-expecting the machine to be broken.

"I'll come," Noah says, pocketing a room key as he

holds the door open for me.

Next to the ice machine, where there should be a pool, lies an empty cement hole covered in dirt and leaves.

"I challenge you to a cannonball competition," I tease, pushing open the creaky metal gate to the pool area.

"No way. If we did that, your road trip would probably end with a hospital visit."

"My cannonballs aren't that bad."

I sink into a nearly broken pool chair, leaning back with a sigh, pretending I'm at a spa. The setting sun warms my face. Though I'm not far from home, this motel feels like another universe entirely.

"No one's ever looked this happy next to a trash-filled, empty pool." Noah leans over the pool's edge to peer inside before taking the seat beside me. Honestly, I'm surprised there are even pool chairs here.

"Skateboarders probably do," I joke, turning to face him. "Everything's so quiet."

Noah tilts his head in confusion as a siren wails in the distance and a car backfires down the street. The timing makes me chuckle.

"Okay, okay. But I still stand by it. I don't hear security talking over their little earpieces. I don't hear footsteps constantly following me. There's usually a buzz—now it's silent."

Noah studies me for a moment, probably thinking I sound like a privileged rich kid complaining about what others would die for.

"So, Southern California?" he says instead.

I grin. "Southern California."

He jumps up, grabs my hand, and pulls me to my feet. "Come on, I saw a computer in the lobby—it probably hasn't been updated since the '90s, but we can still use it."

We head into a small nook off the lobby, dubbed the 'business center,' though I doubt any real business happens here. It must be what dial-up was like—the connecting to the internet takes forever. Eventually, we pull up several routes from Pittsburgh to Southern California.

"Ollie may be getting his road trip experience, but it doesn't seem like a very thrilling one," Noah comments on the different routes, "Lots of boring states."

"Hey, all the states have something to offer," I say, leaning over his shoulder, catching a welcoming scent of citrus—the shampoo from his house. Why does that thought feel like I've stepped into stalker territory?

"Spoken like the first daughter of this country."

I roll my eyes then focus on the three route options on the screen. He's right—each state might have something to offer, but I'm not sure we're heading to any of the country's top sightseeing spots. Honestly, that could be a good thing. Fewer people this way.

"Maybe we should take this route," I say, pointing to the option that heads north, then works its way down. "It goes through Colorado and Utah. Lots of pretty mountains instead of just tumbleweeds."

He clicks the route and hits print. "Plus, that takes us through Vegas. That could be fun."

Noah swivels in his chair to face me. "Why, Miss Ellie, are you saying you're looking forward to Sin City?" He puts a hand on his chest, playing the part of a scandalized southern lady.

"Oh yeah, maybe we could stop by a drive-thru chapel and get married," I tease, grabbing the papers off the printer. I glance at the printed route, wondering how far we'll get before the Secret Service catches up with us.

"Here," Noah says, handing me the room card. "I'm going to ask the front desk about the breakfast they offer. I'm a bit nervous to see it, but if it's decent, it could save us some money."

"That's true," I say, considering his words and how careful we need to be with money since we're living off the cash we pulled. "I can wait for you."

He keeps the card extended. "You better go check on Ollie. We've done more than just get ice—he probably thinks we've become stars in our own horror movie." He waves the card slightly towards me. "I'll be right up."

CHAPTER 8

To no one's surprise, breakfast is a tray of stale muffins and bruised bananas.

We each try to choke one down before piling back into the car, heading toward California.

Ollie claims the front seat this time. Just twenty minutes into the drive, he twists around to face me, grinning like a kid.

"Let's play a game."

"The quiet game?" I ask, only half joking.

"Come on, Els. Classic road trip stuff. This is the only real road trip I'll ever have." He glances from me to Noah, then back.

I sigh. "Fine. Guilt trip accepted. What kind of game?"

"You tell me."

"I'm not exactly a road trip guru either."

"How about the license plate game?" Noah offers, eyes on the road.

Ollie perks up. "Ooo, what's that?"

Noah explains, his tone patient. "We try to spot license plates from as many different states as we can. Whoever finds the most, wins."

"Okay, brilliant, let's play that." Ollie turns to face the window, watching for cars. After a few minutes, he swivels back toward Noah. "Okay, there are not enough cars out here. Let's keep it a running game. What other games are there?"

In the rearview mirror, I catch Noah pressing his lips together, clearly thinking. "We could play Never Have I Ever. That could be a fun way to get to know each other." His eyes flick up, meeting mine in the mirror. We hold the gaze for a beat too long before he turns back to the road.

"I fear everything there is to know about me is already online," Ollie mutters with a sigh.

"No offense, man, but I don't exactly stay up at night googling you."

"Yeah, but I know this one does." He jerks his chin toward me.

I lean forward and smack his shoulder. "That was one time!"

He's referring to when I texted him about that viral rumor—how he supposedly got in trouble for depantsing another student at his fancy private school. Still not sure if it's true.

"Mmhmm," Ollie replies, unconvinced. "Sure, El."

"Okay, fine. How about Would You Rather?" I offer to

change the subject.

Noah and Ollie both nod, so I continue, "Would you rather explore space in a rocket or the ocean in a submarine?"

"Rocket," they say at the exact same time.

"Really?" I laugh, surprised by how quickly they answered. "Why?"

"I think it'd be incredible to see Earth from up there," Ollie says, eyes distant, like he's already imagining it.

"I'd want to meet some aliens," Noah adds, grinning. "Maybe become their king." He turns to Ollie. "Think of the alliance we could forge."

Ollie chuckles as Noah glances at me through the rearview mirror. "What about you, Ellie?"

I press my lips together in thought. "Do I have to pick one?"

Ollie turns in the backseat to face me, eyebrows raised.

"Nope, sorry. I'm not doing either."

"That's not how the game works, El. You have to pick one," he says, like I've never heard of Would You Rather. "Besides, it was your question."

"Fine." I exhale and think for a moment. "The ocean, I guess."

"Why?" Noah chimes in, his eyes catching mine briefly in the rearview mirror.

"Because I had to pick one," I reply flatly, like that settles it.

"Nah," he says, smiling. "You thought that through. What's the real reason?"

I shrug, honest. "I figure death would be faster in a submarine."

Both boys burst out laughing.

"Not true. Your submarine could fail, and you'd just be sitting there, waiting for the oxygen to run out. In space, your rocket could burn up on launch."

I shake my head, already regretting suggesting this question. My mind fills with awful scenarios.

"Or I could go outside in a space suit, and the little cord tethering me to the ship snaps. Then I'm just floating through space, waiting to suffocate." I pause, grimacing. "Actually, no. I take it back. I pick space—because if that happens, I'll just rip off my helmet and get it over with."

Noah raises an eyebrow. "I don't know why both options end in your tragic death, but okay. No space or ocean adventures for you. Noted."

He flashes a half-smile, then turns to Ollie. "Your turn."

Ollie leans back slightly, eyes glinting. "Would you rather be able to touch anything and turn it to gold, or have anyone who looks at you turn to stone?"

He looks at me. "Ellie, you go first."

"I'd rather touch things and have them turn to gold," I say.

"That includes people, too," Ollie points out.

"I know, but I'd have more control over that than if

people turned to stone just by looking at me."

"Yeah, fair point. I'd go with gold, too," Noah says, nodding in agreement.

"I'd choose stone," Ollie replies. "People would avoid me, which isn't always a bad thing. If I could turn things to gold, I'd be expected to use it to make everyone rich. That's a lot of pressure."

"Oh sure," I say with a grin, "why help your people thrive when you can just petrify them instead?"

He chuckles.

"Alright," Noah says, shifting gears, "would you rather be in love but never be able to be together, or never experience love at all?"

"Wow, mate," Ollie whistles. He glances at me, then back at Noah. "That's deep. I think… never experience love. You can't miss what you've never had, right? Besides, in my world, a love match isn't always on the table anyway."

"Hey!" I cut in, nudging him. "I told you, if we're both still single at thirty, we're getting married. That would totally be a love match."

Ollie turns back to me with a charming smile.

"I think my country might not be thrilled if their king married an American. And besides, you're my best friend. I can't imagine us… You know"—he hesitates—"doing what needs to be done to have an heir."

I gasp, mock-offended, and give his shoulder a light punch.

"Wow. Rude! Fine."

I pivot toward Noah with theatrical flair.

"Noah, it seems I've just lost my backup plan. So, hear me out. If neither of us is married by thirty—wait, scratch that. We're not royal, no heirs needed, so let's say thirty-five—do you want to get married? Or does the thought of continuing the Hart bloodline with me make you physically ill?"

"Hey!" Ollie objects turning towards me, but I ignore him.

Noah's hands tighten on the steering wheel, his knuckles whitening.

Oh. Wow. Okay then.

Apparently, the idea of having children with me is truly revolting.

Mental note: pencil in some time for some serious self-reflection.

"Just think about it," I say quickly, trying to save him from answering and myself from the embarrassment of hearing his obvious reply. "I'd choose being in love but not being able to be together."

"Tragic," Ollie mutters.

I shrug. "Everyone loves a forbidden romance, right? Think of Jack and Rose."

"Or Romeo and Juliet," Noah adds quietly, giving a small nod. "I'd pick the same. I'd rather experience love, even if it's forbidden."

His eyes meet mine through the rearview mirror, and my stomach flips like we've just crested a steep hill.

"Misery!" Ollie suddenly shouts, making both Noah and me jump. "Yes! First state down."

"What was it?" I glance at the car we just passed and realize he's still playing the license plate game.

"Misery."

"It's pronounced Missouri... but honestly, close enough," Noah says with a low chuckle that sends warm vibrations through me.

Oh no. I might be in trouble.

CHAPTER 9

We're somewhere near the Indiana border, parked at a gas station. My legs are stiff from hours in the car, and I'm dying to stretch—plus, I need snacks.

As I step out of the restroom, I spot Ollie in the chip aisle. He's deep in conversation with two girls.

"You look so familiar," one of them says, squinting at him with a little too much interest.

I freeze. Do I need to jump in before they recognize him—or worse, both of us?

I duck into the next aisle and pretend to be fascinated by a wall of gum while I eavesdrop.

"Guess I just have one of those faces," Ollie replies, smooth as ever. I can hear the smile in his voice. Of course, he's enjoying this.

"Trust me," the girl giggles, "no one around here has a face like yours. Or an accent like that."

Another girl casually rests her hand on Ollie's arm. I glance around, silently hoping no one else is paying attention. That's when I spot it—right next to the register, a tabloid cover with photos of both Ollie and me arriving separately at the gala the other night. Classic. The press loves nothing more than twisting a friendship into a fairytale romance. A boy and a girl can't just be friends.

"Wait…" one girl, who's been scrolling on her phone, looks up sharply. "You're Prince Oliver?"

She doesn't whisper. Of course not. Her voice cuts through the store like a knife.

More gasps.

"What? You're Prince Oliver? What are you doing in the middle of nowhere, Indiana?"

That's my cue.

I stride over and grab Ollie's arm. "We need to go. Now." I give the group a tight smile. "Sorry to steal him away, ladies."

I try to keep my voice light, but panic coils tight in my gut. They've seen us, and they'll post it—probably already alerting the Secret Service with their polished black SUVs.

"Wait!" One of them calls after us, but I don't look back.

We rush toward the door just as Noah pushes it open.

"Hey, just let me run to the restroom and–"

"Nope. Hold it." I press a hand to his chest and steer him right back outside.

"What happened?" Noah straightens, instantly alert, guiding us toward the car.

"Ask Prince Charming," I mutter, sliding into the passenger seat while Ollie climbs into the back.

Sure enough, the girls trail us, phones out, snapping pictures. We're so done for.

Noah throws the car in reverse. As much as I want him to peel out like he's auditioning for *Fast and Furious*, he pulls away at a perfectly normal speed.

I tilt my head back against the seat, staring at the roof. Breathe. Just breathe.

"What happened?" Noah asks again.

"Nothing," Ollie says, poking his head between the seats. "I was just talking to some girls, and one of them recognized me." He glances at me, sheepish. "El, I'm sorry."

I don't answer, closing my eyes. We lasted longer than I thought—just when it felt like we might actually pull this off.

"Ellie?" Noah's voice cuts through the silence.

"They got a picture of our car at the gas station. We've probably got two hours, max, before the Secret Service finds us."

Ollie curses under his breath. Noah's knuckles whiten on the steering wheel as he keeps his focus on the road.

Miles pass in tense silence before Noah finally breaks it. "Okay, I know things are chaotic and I'm really sorry, but…I have to pee."

He veers off at the next exit and pulls into a small

station, choosing a spot away from the other cars.

"Two minutes," he says, already out the door and hurrying inside.

Once we're back on the road, I can't take my eyes off the side mirror. I'm waiting for black SUVs, or even the local police, to come up behind us. We've been silent since Noah returned from the restroom. Not sure what there is to say anymore—our road trip clock is literally counting down.

"Michigan." Ollie leans forward, pointing at a license plate passing us. That breaks the tension, and in true Ollie fashion, it makes us laugh.

The farther we get down the road, the more I can relax without spotting any security. We're a couple of hours outside Chicago when we decide to stop for the night. We find another motel—still no Four Seasons, but at least not a horror movie set like the last one. All the sign's letters are there, and the neon isn't flickering. Standards aren't exactly high on this trip.

It wasn't exactly a packed day but we all climb into our beds without much conversation. Noah sleeps on his makeshift bed on the floor. I try not to think about how it's made from the duvets I know they never wash. I don't want to imagine what's lurking in the fibers of the ugly red carpet beneath him.

The room is pitch dark. Ollie lies in the bed beside me, his breathing heavy but steady. I wish I could fall asleep as easily as he does. I try counting sheep, but every noise outside convinces me that Marks and his team are about to burst in and drag me away.

I'm just starting to drift off when Noah bolts upright at the foot of the bed.

My heart pounds as he leaps onto the bed, stirring Ollie beside us, though he seems still asleep.

"Something touched me!" Noah whisper-yells. "No, wait—not even touched. Something crawled across me!"

I let out a surprised giggle, not expecting this level of panic from him. Leaning over, I flick on the bedside lamp. "If it's a mouse, I swear we're burning this place down."

I crawl to the side of the bed, eyes scanning his rumpled blankets for any movement.

"Noah! Noah! Noah!" I swat his arm as my heart rockets. Then I point at the wall. "There! Oh my gosh, get it!"

A massive cockroach crawls up the wall, its antennae twitching like a warning. I cling to Noah's arm like the rodent-sized bug is a direct threat to my safety.

Noah rises slowly, his movements careful and precise, so he doesn't scare it off. He lifts his shoe, ready to strike. The walls here are paper-thin, so anyone in the next room is about to get a rude wake-up call.

Noah is just about to smash it and end my misery when the bug takes flight.

I scream, diving under the blankets like they'll somehow keep me safe. Ollie jerks upright in bed, clearly confused — probably convinced we're being murdered.

Our neighbors might not have had a bug killed on our shared wall, but my scream, sounding like a murder scene, definitely alerted someone.

"It can fly? Why can it fly?" I shriek from beneath the covers. "Is this a nightmare? Noah, kill it, please!"

I lowered my blanket slowly to peek out, only for Noah to meet my eyes and widen his own.

"Don't. Move."

It's not reassuring, not even a little. In fact, it's probably one of the worst things he could say right now. I shriek again, burying myself deeper under the blanket. "It touched me! I felt it touch me!"

"It didn't touch you," Ollie laughs. "It was way above you on the wall."

I refuse to come out from under the blanket until one of them confirms it's safe. I hear shuffling footsteps, a few failed attempts, then finally a loud, satisfying whack.

Ollie cheers, and I cautiously pull the blankets down to see Noah holding a tissue-wrapped corpse like a trophy.

"What if it had a family watching?" Ollie asks as Noah flushes the tissue down the toilet. "Now they're probably plotting revenge against us."

I hurl a pillow at Ollie's face. He bats it away with a laugh. "That's not funny!"

"Don't worry, Ellie." Noah scans the room like he's addressing an invisible bug mafia. "That was just a warning. Be sure to tell your friends." He calls out to the room.

Noah turns his attention back to us with a satisfied nod

before he flips the lamp off.

"Wait." I grab his arm before he can walk away. "You're not seriously going back to the floor, are you?"

The room is dark, so I lean over and turn the light back on. Both Ollie and Noah are staring at me. I already felt bad that Noah was sleeping on the floor, but now? After the flying cockroach of doom? No way. Who knows what's next?

A mouse?

A stinkbug?

A raccoon?

"Yeah," he says, gently pulling free of my grip. "I was planning on it."

He turns the light off again.

I flick it right back on.

He sighs, long and weary, like I'm the final boss battle in a game he's losing.

"I'll sleep with Ollie," I announce, leaping across the beds before either of them can object. I scramble onto Ollie's mattress like the floor is lava, refusing to let even a toe graze the cursed carpet.

"It's fine. I'm fine."

"Well, I'm already comfy, so I guess that bed's going to be empty while you sacrifice yourself to whatever other horror lives in this place," I say, burrowing into the blankets with a theatrical sigh.

Noah smirks and flops back onto his duvet. "Ah, yes,

the floor bed. Luxurious. I've always dreamed of sleeping somewhere mildly cursed and full of cockroach ghosts."

"Don't say cockroach ghosts! Now that's all I'm going to be thinking about." I sit up on my elbows to glare at him.

"Mate," Ollie mumbles, rubbing his eyes, "it's easier for all of us if you just get in the bed."

Noah lifts his hands in surrender and climbs into the empty mattress. I roll onto my side to face him, and he mirrors me. His eyes narrow, tired and amused, like he can't believe I actually won.

I grin, lean over, and flick off the lamp.

"Sweet dreams."

CHAPTER 10

L ook!" I jump into the backseat, waving a flyer I grabbed from the gas station counter.

Both boys turn. Ollie snatches the bag of Sour Patch Kids I just bought.

"American candy is something else," he mutters, tossing one in his mouth.

Noah's eyes stay on the flyer. "What did you find?"

"There's a football game tonight!"

"It's football season. There are probably a dozen games tonight," Noah says, smirking.

"You know what I mean. Here, in this town. Let's go!"

"Yes!" Ollie's grin widens. "I want to watch the sport that is so poorly named in person."

"I don't know, guys. It's not even lunchtime. We've still got a lot of road to cover."

"Come on, Noah." I lean forward, hooking my arm around his, and snuggle up with exaggerated innocence. I bat my lashes like I've practiced. "It's about the journey, not the destination."

Ollie laughs and leans over the console, his head nearly brushing mine.

"Yeah mate, let's live, laugh, love."

"Fine," Noah sighs, like we've just asked him to smuggle a piano, not watch a football game. "If we go to this game, will you two stop quoting cheesy home décor signs?"

"Okay, okay!" I lean back with my hands up in surrender. "Just keep calm and carry on."

Noah shakes his head, biting back a smile as he shifts gears and turns toward town instead of the freeway.

"You know," I say, tugging at the collar of Leah's sweatshirt, "we need clothes that don't scream Runaway First Daughter and Prince on Holiday."

Noah meets my eyes in the rearview mirror, then glances at Ollie slouched in the passenger seat, wearing his hoodie.

"Hey, you've got Leah's clothes on and Ollie's got mine. You're blending in just fine."

"Yeah, maybe," I say, wrinkling my nose. "But I have a strong feeling this car's going to smell like regret if we stay in these clothes too long."

That earns a nod in agreement from Noah. At last.

We drive slowly down Main Street until we spot a small thrift store tucked between a laundromat and an old diner. Noah pulls into the back lot, which is mercifully empty except for one car—probably an employee's.

Inside, the place is a labyrinth of color and chaos, overflowing with multicolored racks and mismatched hangers. It feels like the entire town has refused to throw out a single item of clothing, choosing instead to donate every memory-laced thread here.

The air carries a cocktail of old perfume, stale cardboard, and something musty I'd rather not identify.

But I don't care. It's beautiful.

Not beautiful like the White House—sterile, curated, important. This place is the opposite. Beautiful in the way only something alive and untamed can be.

Everything here hums with history. A denim jacket hand-embroidered with wildflowers. Flared jeans with someone's name scrawled in Sharpie across the waistband. An emerald velvet dress, its sleeves fraying and its tiny round buttons holding on for dear life.

That's the one that stops me.

It's exactly the kind of dress I used to sketch in the margins of my econ notes, back when I dreamed about what I'd wear if headlines and dress codes weren't part of the equation. I trail my fingers over the buttons like they're artifacts from a life I still want. Already, my mind is reworking the cut—shortening the hem, cinching the bodice, maybe swapping in a silk lining.

"I'm in love," I whisper.

Across the aisle, Ollie is buried halfway into a rack of polyester suits. He pulls out a mint-green tux jacket with the reverence of someone unearthing treasure. "If I don't wear this to my wedding someday, I'll have failed myself.”

I let out a laugh and shake my head. “That would definitely be a royal wedding for the history books.”

Noah appears beside me, holding up a neon orange windbreaker with mock seriousness. “Is this giving traffic cone to you?”

I grin, fingers still brushing the delicate buttons on the dress.

“That one’s actually kind of cool,” he says, nodding toward the gown, his voice casual but observant.

I shrug, masking how completely obsessed I am with it. “I’d never be allowed to wear something like this back home.”

“Good thing you’re not home,” Noah says simply, taking the dress off the rack and handing it to me.

I take it carefully, like it might shatter in my hands.

Ollie appears beside us out of nowhere, now wearing the mint tux and a top hat, I’m sure he didn’t have five minutes ago. “Did I miss a heartfelt moment?” He studies our faces, then grins. “I have an idea. Let’s make this a competition!”

Noah lifts an eyebrow. “What kind of competition?”

“Only the most important showdown in British-American history,” Ollie declares. “Fashion Olympics. No rules. Winner gets snack veto power for twenty-four hours.”

I smirk. “You’re on.”

Fifteen minutes later, we step out of the dressing rooms like contestants on the weirdest runway Iowa has ever seen. Ollie's still in the mint tux but has added a fanny pack and a pair of cowboy boots. Noah's wearing a bedazzled denim jacket over a Teenage Mutant Ninja Turtles tee, topped off with oversized, heart-shaped sunglasses he insists "speak to his soul."

And me? I'm in the frayed velvet dress, a sequined cape I found in the kids' section, and—because I couldn't resist—light-up sneakers that somehow fit.

We strike a pose in front of a dressing room mirror, a long crack running down the center like it's barely holding itself together.

Noah smirks at me in the reflection, his eyes lingering just a second longer than they probably should. But I don't find it creepy. In fact, I actually like it. I like being under his gaze with that look of…adoration.

"You look…" he says, voice low.

He trails off. I turn to face him, pulse quickening.

"Yeah?" I ask, aiming for casual but hearing the hope in my own voice.

He clears his throat.

"…Like you're finally getting to be you."

For a moment, the world shifts—just a fraction—but enough to make my chest ache in that painful, good way. My cheeks burn.

And then Ollie swoops in, tossing a pink feather boa around my neck.

"Okay, sentimental time's over," he announces. "We've got a winner with high honors to decide."

I can't stop looking at myself in the mirror, one finger trailing the hem of the dress as ideas start to sketch themselves in my mind.

Maybe I don't just love wearing clothes like this.

Maybe I want to make them.

"I vote Ellie," Noah says, with no hesitation.

"Do I get to vote for myself?" Ollie asks.

"No," Noah shoots back immediately.

"Fine," Ollie sighs, disappointed by this rule. "I vote Ellie too."

"Yay! Snack power is mine!" I declare, arms in the air like some Disney villain.

"For the record, you still need to vote," Ollie adds, striking a dramatic pose.

"Noah," I start deceivingly with a pause, which works because Ollie gasps in mock betrayal. "I'm sorry," I continue with a smirk, "but I'm going to have to vote Ollie."

Ollie cheers. Noah laughs.

"I get it," Noah says, gesturing at Ollie, "hard to pass up a prince in a mint-green tux and fanny pack."

"Okay, but now we need to focus on finding clothes appropriate for a football game," I say, heading toward a nearby rack.

"I'm keeping the cowboy boots," Ollie announces, already striding toward a row of plaid flannels.

"You're getting the dress, right?" Noah asks, appearing beside me.

"Nah, this isn't really giving 'football game,'" I say.

"Maybe not, but you'll regret it if you don't," Noah replies, heading towards a rack of long-sleeve shirts.

He's right. I can't imagine leaving this dress behind.

Twenty minutes later, we check out. Noah didn't need any 'normal' clothes, so Ollie and I kept it simple — a few pairs of jeans, shirts, a jacket, and sneakers. I added a pair of sunglasses; Ollie, of course, kept his cowboy boots and a baseball hat with the John Deere logo.

"You look ridiculous," I say, laughing as we climb into the car.

Ollie flips down the sun visor and checks his reflection. "Come on, it's the ultimate undercover disguise. No one would ever guess I'm a prince."

"Never thought you'd be cosplaying a country boy." I swat at his hat, knocking it askew.

"Cosplaying? This isn't cosplaying, Ellie. This is my new identity."

"Oh really? Planning to drive a tractor to your coronation?"

"Can you just let me have fun for, like, five minutes?" He asks, mock-annoyed.

We stop to eat at the cutest small-town diner, the kind

that makes me feel like I've stepped onto a Hallmark movie set. Then we head towards the high school.

"Just another night watching the greatest game with the most accurate name," Ollie says, slipping into an American accent as we get our hands stamped at the entrance to show we've paid.

"Okay, *Chad*." I give him a look — he's not exactly subtle.

"I don't know, Chad sounds like a frat boy name, and he's anything but a frat boy right now."

I turn to smile at Noah and freeze, surprised by how close he is. He's like some magnetic force — I don't want to step away.

"Y'all see that there truck? Now that's got some grind," Ollie says, breaking whatever hypnotic trance Noah had me under.

I roll my eyes playfully, grab Ollie's wrist, and pull him through the entrance gates toward the bleachers.

CHAPTER 11

The bright stadium lights cast a yellow glow over the field, the crowd buzzing with excitement. It's loud, louder than I expected, louder than anything I've ever really been allowed to be part of.

We find seats near the top of the bleachers, and I soak it all in. We blend into the crowd, and Ollie has fully embraced his country-boy act—though he hasn't a clue what he's talking about. He insists we call him Robby, which, honestly, suits him better than Chad.

I grip the edge of the bleacher, eyes darting around, half-expecting someone to spot that I don't belong here and drag me back to my perfectly curated, perfectly safe First Daughter bubble.

Then there's Noah.

Noah sits beside me, legs stretched out, hands clasped between his knees, trying to look casual but practically buzzing with nervous energy. When I glance at him, he's already watching me.

I give him a reassuring smile. "Come on, Noah. Friday night football? This is American culture at its peak. You know, 'clear eyes, full hearts, can't lose'—that kind of thing."

The student section erupts into cheers, the band launching into a fight song I don't know.

Noah tilts his head, voice low. "Whatever you say, *Friday Night Lights*," he jokes, pointing out my quote.

I wish I could freeze this moment. This game is everything I missed by not going to a public high school, but saw on some of my favorite shows. The stands are awash in school colors, cheerleaders lead the student section's cheers from the track, and the whole town acts like it's the Super Bowl, not just a hometown game.

"So, what do you think? Worth the risk?"

I should say I don't know yet—still figuring out if this reckless little rebellion of ours was a mistake. But instead, I look at the packed bleachers, the players crashing into each other on the field, and the way Noah watches me like my answer actually matters.

"Yeah, absolutely worth the risk."

And I really believe it. I've travelled the country, met world leaders, yet here at a small-town football game in Iowa, I'm not sure I've ever been happier.

The crowd rises as the final seconds tick down, pushing the game into overtime.

"Wow," I sigh, sinking back into my seat, "The only thing that would make this better is nachos."

"Let's do it. I could eat," Noah says, pulling me to my feet.

I don't object, but Ollie chooses to stay, eyes on the band performing nearby.

We join the queue at the concessions—a small building tucked behind the bleachers. My gaze drifts over the crowd: folks grabbing food, groups of teens hanging out behind the stands, old couples holding hands in school colors.

Then I spot familiar faces—black suits standing out sharply against the casual crowd.

Just like that, my joy evaporates.

I press my palms against Noah's chest and shove us out of line.

"What is it?" he asks, grabbing my hands and squeezing them. His eyes lock onto mine, sharp and alert.

I glance over his shoulder and spot familiar suits weaving through the crowd—my security detail.

"They're here," I say, voice tight. My eyes track the agents closing in. How did they find us? No one else has noticed us, or at least I didn't see anyone looking at us with recognition. Who could have tipped security off?

I grip Noah's hands, trying to pull us the other way, but I barely get two steps before more suits materialize. We're surrounded.

I freeze, hands falling to my sides. That's it. Game over. The night was perfect—until now.

"Ellie," Noah says my name like an apology, like he already knows this is the end of the road.

Out of the corner of my eye, I catch two teens making out like she's sending him off to war. They don't care who's watching. It's so painfully intimate, I have to look away—but then something clicks.

I glance at the couple again. Then back to Noah.

A flash of memory: Ollie, on the gala night. What he said about PDA when awkwardly nuzzled in my neck.

"Kiss me," I blurt, grabbing Noah's hand.

"What?" He stares at me like I've just asked him to jump off the Empire State Building.

I don't have time to dissect the panic in his eyes. I'll definitely obsess over it later.

Instead, I fist the front of his T-shirt and pull him closer.

"People hate PDA," I whisper, and before he can object, I crash my mouth into his.

It takes a second, but then he kisses me back. And when he does, I melt into it like slipping under the covers on a winter night. Everything else disappears.

His hands come up to cradle my face, and I rise onto my toes to meet him. The guards might've already passed, but I'm not about to look. I don't want this kiss to end.

BOOM.

We spring apart as the sky lights up green.

Another boom—red this time.

Noah instinctively steps in front of me, tense and protective—until he realizes it's only fireworks.

"You okay?" he asks, eyes scanning my face, like he's trying to figure out whether I've been shot or kissed senseless.

"Oh sure," I say, breathless. "Your kiss just caused literal fireworks."

I try to sound casual, but my heart's still thudding as I glance around. No sign of the guards.

The game seems to be over, which is honestly perfect timing.

"We need to find Ollie and get out of here," I say.

We weave through the crowd and back into the bleachers. Ollie's still in his seat, chatting with someone behind him.

"Hey, sorry to interrupt," I say, sliding in beside him, keeping my tone light but urgent. "We need to go. Now."

Ollie meets my eyes. There's a beat of silent understanding. He stands, but before we can slip away, the guy behind him tilts his head and studies me.

"You look familiar."

I freeze. I don't have to look to know Ollie and Noah have gone tense beside me.

"I work at the market down the street," I say quickly, smoothly, calling up the image of the grocery store we passed earlier by the diner. "Maybe you've seen me there? Do you have kids? Maybe one graduated with me?"

"Only a grandson—he's out there." The man nods toward the field, where students now spill across the grass, laughing and hugging. "But I do shop at Main Street Market. Must be it."

I loop my fingers around Ollie's arm, offering an easy smile. "That's probably it. Hope to see you next time you're in. We've got a two-for-one chili deal this week."

He chuckles, nodding, and Ollie gives a polite goodbye as we trail behind Noah down the bleachers.

"Chili?" Ollie laughs, sliding his arm around my shoulders. "Let's hope he doesn't show up just for that."

I smile back, but the warmth fades fast.

Suits. At least half a dozen in the parking lot. Scanning windshields. Some cars are stopping.

"That's for you guys, right?" Noah mutters.

I nod, tight-lipped. "Well, Ollie, looks like we get to snuggle while we get smuggled."

"No. Absolutely not," Noah snaps. "I am not stuffing the future king and America's princess in my trunk."

Princess.

The word hits me like a slap—Dad.

He must be worried sick. I'll call him on the burner as soon as we're safe.

"We don't have a choice," Ollie mutters, already scanning the area. Then, without waiting, he climbs into the trunk.

Noah turns to me, his expression tight, silently begging me not to follow. But we're out of time, and we both know it.

"Come on, Ellie Belly," Ollie calls softly, poking his head back out.

I slide in beside him. Noah exhales, defeated. He gives one last look around, then shuts the trunk gently.

Darkness swallows us whole.

The car jolts forward. I reach for Ollie's hand and grip it tight. Every breath feels like it echoes. I try to slow it, convinced they'll hear us somehow.

The car stops. Voices filter in through the trunk. My heart leaps into my throat.

Still holding on, we freeze.

The car starts again.

Time inside the trunk is elastic, bending and stretching with each breath. Minutes pass—or maybe seconds—until the car stops once more.

A door creaks open, then the trunk.

Noah stands there, backlit by a sky littered with stars.

For a second, all I can think about is what it would feel like to live somewhere you could actually see the stars? The night wraps around him like a painting, the constellations casting him in quiet glory. I'm almost breathless.

He reaches in and grabs my hand. I climb out, inhaling the crisp night air.

"Come on," he says. "Let's get you two out of here. We are never doing that again."

"You're so uptight. Kids sneak into places like this all

the time."

"Yeah, well, they're not the president's daughter or the prince of England."

"Hey!" Ollie hops out. "I'm not a prince. I'm just country boy Robby."

"And I'm Ellie, your friendly neighborhood grocery store cashier. Did you hear about our chili deal?"

"Never. Again," Noah says, pointing at both of us like a dad scolding toddlers.

He may hate how it happened, but it worked. We're safe.

Another day on the road. Another memory.

And honestly?

Today was perfect.

CHAPTER 12

When we're back on the road the next morning, I remember the promise I made to myself last night—to call Dad. I wait until we pull over for a bathroom break before asking Noah for his burner.

I wander over to a picnic table near the edge of the lot and sit. The phone feels heavier than it should in my hand. I stare at the keypad, thumb hovering. Instead of dialing Dad, I press the other number I have memorized.

It rings three times before a rushed voice answers.

"Grant speaking."

"Hey Grant, it's your favorite little sister."

There's a long, theatrical sigh on the other end. Classic. I roll my eyes hard enough to see my own brain.

"Ellie." His voice is flat. Cold. Like he's already bracing for impact.

Regret creeps in fast and settles in my gut. This was a mistake.

"Great to hear from you, too, big bro."

"What are you thinking? Are you nuts?"

I hear a door slam behind him, and I picture him stepping out of some glass-walled conference room, probably fresh off helping some powerful CEO crush a harmless underdog in court. Classic Grant.

"Currently? Yeah, calling you might not be in my top ten decisions. But guess what? I'm alive. I'm safe. And here's the wildest part—I went to a football game. Yep. Better alert the authorities."

"You do realize this is an election year, right?" His voice sharpens. "Do you think Dad needs this right now? Wondering where in the world you are when he's supposed to be campaigning? And not just that, Eleanor. You're with the heir to England. Do you have any idea what this looks like? You could be facing charges— kidnapping, harboring a runaway, or whatever else their lawyers cook up. They're not going to just let this slide."

"I'm not going to be charged with kidnapping Ollie!" I snap, louder than I meant to. Frustration bubbles to the surface.

"Sure. Because obviously, you know the law better than I do." His sarcasm is ice-cold. "Ellie, I'm trying to help you. Stop being so... stupid."

"Like you and your frat buddies didn't do worse? Stop pretending you're the perfect son. We left a gala, we're on a road trip, and I'm checking in like a responsible adult. Everything's fine, okay? I was hoping you'd have my back."

"Don't turn this on me, El. You're being selfish."

"You probably have some single mother to evict or whatever, so I'll let you go. Great talking to you, Grant," I say, voice dripping with sarcasm as I hang up.

Heat rises in my chest, sharp and sour. No one knows how to push my buttons faster than Grant. He's ten years older and never lived in the White House, or even the Governor's mansion. He's always had pressure, sure, but nothing like the relentless spotlight I've grown up under.

I plop into the back seat and shut the door a little harder than necessary. Honestly, it feels good to let something out.

Up front, Ollie's mid-story, animatedly telling Noah about the time we tried to bake a cake in the White House kitchen and accidentally set off the fire alarm. His hands are probably flying everywhere like they always do when he's reliving our chaos.

I keep my eyes fixed on the window, even though I can feel Noah watching me through the rearview mirror as we merge back onto the road.

"We're banned from making anything in the kitchen now, huh, Els?" Ollie says. It's more of a statement than a question, so I don't bother responding.

I hear him shift in his seat, the rustle of fabric, and I know he's turning around to look at me.

"Els, you alright? Phone call with Grant not go over well?"

Nope. It definitely didn't. Now I just feel grumpy and

raw. If I open my mouth now, I know the mood will leak out and ruin the air around us. They don't deserve that.

So I stay quiet.

"Hello?" Ollie says. I glance over at him.

"Oh, good, you can hear me. For a second there, I thought I might be a ghost."

I roll my eyes and turn back to the window.

"Oh. Maybe I am a ghost. Noah, can you hear me, mate?"

Noah humors him with a soft "mmhmm."

A seatbelt clicks. Before I can fully process it, Ollie is climbing over the console.

"Woah! Ollie!"

"What are you doing?" Noah and I say at the same time.

Ollie flops into the middle seat, buckles in, and grins at me. "Hi."

"Ollie, you're the heir to a country. You absolutely cannot be climbing around in a moving car."

"What? I missed my best friend." He throws his arms around me, pulling me into a suffocating hug. After a moment, he eases off slightly but keeps one arm looped around my shoulders.

"Noah, with both of us back here, it's kind of like you're our chauffeur."

"I am your chauffeur," Noah replies flatly.

"No, like you're Nigel. He's usually my driver." Ollie

claps a few times, adopting a mock-posh tone. "Oh, driver, make haste!"

I can't help it—I giggle. The corner of Noah's mouth twitches upward as he mutters something under his breath about royalty.

"Wait, have you really told your driver to 'make haste'?" Noah asks, slipping into a ridiculously exaggerated British accent to impersonate Ollie. It only makes me laugh harder.

"You sound like you walked straight out of a Jane Austen novel."

Just like that, the call with Grant fades into the background. It always happens like this. Ollie flips my mood like a switch. And now, with Noah helping him, I don't stand a chance.

I've spent a lifetime being irritated with my brother. I'm not going to let it ruin this moment.

However, as if there's something in the air today, I only realize something's wrong when a few hours later Ollie halts mid-step in the gas station snack aisle. His hand freezes above a bag of sour gummy worms.

My eyes follow his stare to the checkout counter. A glossy tabloid, angled for maximum visibility, practically screams at us in bold capital letters:

WILD CHILD OF WINDSOR: Inside the Palace Party Years – Oliver Unleashed!

Exclusive excerpts from a former royal staffer's scandalous memoir!

Front and center is a grainy photo of Ollie from a few years back—shirtless, sun-dazed, swim-trunked, gripping a bottle of champagne like it's an Olympic torch. He's grinning at nothing in particular, completely unaware of the camera, the moment, the fallout.

"Wow," I murmur. "You look... hydrated."

He doesn't laugh. Not even a flicker of a smile.

I glance at him again. His jaw is locked tight, but his fingers betray him, curling slowly into a fist at his side. He snatches the tabloid off the rack and flips it open with a sharp rustle.

I catch a glimpse of one of the excerpts:

"We were instructed never to question Prince Oliver's after-hours escapades. He often arrived at breakfast still smelling of champagne and Chanel..."

"You smell like that now," I say, trying to lighten the mood. It falls flat.

He tosses the magazine back like it burned him.

"It's exaggerated," he mutters. "All of it. I mean—yes, I went to parties, but this whole narrative that I'm some royal trainwreck—"

"Ollie..."

"They want me to be a disaster," he snaps, eyes flashing. "Because it's easier to write off a future king than to ask if maybe the crown itself is what's broken."

His voice rises, too loud now. The guy at the counter glances up. I tug Ollie gently toward the doors, steering us away from the register.

Outside, the air is sharp and cool. Ollie drags a hand through his hair, pacing tight circles like a storm wound too tight.

"I'm trying, Ellie. I really am. Trying to be better than the version they plastered across the tabloids. That was years ago—back when I was still at Eton. But maybe it doesn't matter. Maybe the public has already decided who I am. Maybe I'll never be anything more than that spoiled teenage prince."

I step in front of him, halting his steps. "You're not a headline, Ollie. You're not some cautionary tale with a scandalous title."

He doesn't answer. I press further.

"You're the guy who brings me peanut butter M&M's just because they're my favorite. The guy who saw something online about 'romanticizing your life' and actually did it. You're not reckless. You're romantic."

His expression flickers—like he doesn't quite believe it yet, but wants to.

"And hey," I say, nudging his arm, "for what it's worth, you look great in that photo."

Finally, a breath of a laugh escapes. "I was three martinis deep and doing the Macarena on a yacht."

"Right. So regal."

He exhales slowly. "This book's going to blow up."

"Yeah, probably. But you need to be louder," I tell him.

"Not with rage or press statements—by showing them who you are now. Not the version sold in a memoir, but the one you're still writing."

He looks at me for a long moment. Then he nods, like maybe that version is still within reach.

I hook my arm through his as we walk back to the car. Without looking back, he tosses the tabloid into the nearest trash can.

"You sound like a speechwriter, you know?"

I smirk. "Well, I am the president's daughter. It's kind of in my DNA."

"Nah. Your dad has people for that. This is all you, always knowing the right thing to say."

CHAPTER 13

The next morning, I'm determined to send nothing but good vibes into the universe after yesterday's emotional rollercoaster with Ollie. For a while, everything runs smoothly. Ollie's playing his license plate game solo, flipping through radio stations until we land on songs we all know, and I'm quietly trying to learn anything I can about Noah.

But the peace doesn't last long.

A few hours into the drive, the car jerks slightly. I sit up straighter, glancing into the side-view mirror to see if we hit something.

Another jolt. This one is less intense.

Then another.

I glance at Noah. His eyes are locked on the dashboard, eyebrows pulled together in tight concentration. I lean toward him, trying to catch a glimpse of whatever has his attention as he flips the blinker on and guides us to the side of the road.

"I'm guessing cars don't normally do this kind of thing in the States?"

Ollie leans forward, wedging his head between our seats. I press a hand to his forehead and gently push him back.

"Cars nowhere do this kind of thing." I glance at Noah. "What is it?"

He drags a hand through his hair, the gesture caught somewhere between concentration and frustration.

"I'm not sure." He pulls his phone from his pocket, frowning at the screen like it just betrayed him, then tosses it into the cup holder. "Why can't they make burner phones with internet?"

It's rhetorical, so I stay quiet.

He turns to us, his eyes flicking between me and Ollie. "Either of you know anything about cars?"

The look on his face borders on desperate, as if hoping one of us has a background in auto mechanics.

"I know how to race them," Ollie offers brightly.

"Of course you do," I mutter.

"Don't ask me." I raise my hands in surrender. "I always call my dad for this stuff, and that's not an option. I did learn how to change a tire once. Could it be that?"

He shakes his head, eyes narrowing at the dashboard. "No, there are lights on, and I have no clue what they mean."

I pop open the glovebox, hoping for a manual. It's stuffed with takeout napkins and crumpled receipts, but at the very bottom, I find it. I unbuckle and lean toward

Noah, squinting to match the glowing icons on the dash with the faded diagrams in the booklet.

"Can you pop the hood?" I ask, cracking open my door.

Before I can step out, Noah grabs my arm to stop me. "You're not getting out on a busy road."

I glance at him, then out the window. A few cars pass, but it's hardly gridlocked.

"Whatever it is, I'll check," he says, leaning down to pull the hood release.

"I think it's engine-related," he adds, frowning at the warning lights. "But I've got no idea what exactly."

He presses his palms against his eyes and takes a few deep breaths. "Alright, well, is there a number for roadside assistance?"

He grabs the phone he had tossed aside as I flip through the manual, hunting for a number to call.

We're stranded about twenty miles from a small town. Thankfully, one with an open body shop that agrees to tow us in. The place is called Hank's, and, unsurprisingly, it's run by a cute old man named Hank.

The small waiting room smells like rubber, and the harsh fluorescent lights make it feel more like a dentist's office than a garage. I lean my head back against the wall and exhale slowly while we wait to find out if it's a quick fix.

Across the room, a wire magazine rack catches my eye. At first glance, it's the usual tabloid fluff. But then I see them—familiar faces staring back at me.

"Oh no," I whisper.

I snatch the magazine and stare at the cover in horror before flipping it open, frantically searching for the article.

"What is it?" Ollie asks from behind me.

I don't answer right away. Instead, I flip through the magazine until I land on the page I've been searching for.

"Is that what I think it is?" He asks, suddenly now beside me, making me jump. He doesn't acknowledge my flinch. Instead, he points to the glossy spread.

There, for the world to see, is a photo of the two of us in Indiana beneath the headline: Diplomatic Flirting? The First Daughter and the Prince's Romantic Connection.

"If you think it's an article about how we're madly in love, then yeah. It's exactly what you think it is."

Ollie leans in to study the page more closely, then pulls back and glances at me. "Well, at least they picked some flattering photos."

"Ollie!" I swat his arm. "This is serious."

"Why? The media already thinks we're dating. Who cares?"

"It's so annoying," I grumble, snapping the magazine shut and handing it to him a bit too forcefully. At least it's not the one about his family's memoir. "I'm going to find the restroom."

I head down the narrow hallway, following the signs, but pause when I notice a door at the end. Through its small window, I see the garage.

Something tugs at me.

I push open the door and step inside. Hank is hunched over, tinkering beneath the hood of a car. I quietly slide up beside him.

"Hi, Hank. How's it looking?"

"Oh, hi, sweetie." He glances at me, then places his hands on his hips and takes a step back. "Looks like we need to replace a few parts. I've got most of them, but there's one I'll need to order in. Just checking that everything else is still in good shape."

"Do you mind if I watch?" I lean in toward the engine, eager to learn something more useful than just changing a tire.

Hank agrees and I lose track of how long I've been back in the garage with Hank when I hear Noah's voice cutting through the air, sharp and urgent.

"Eleanor!"

"In here, Noah," I call, still crouched over the engine as I tighten a bolt.

He rushes in, and I glance at him before turning back to the car.

"Hank's just showing me a few things—like how to check a car's oil." I flash a proud smile at Hank, but when I look back at Noah, it fades.

His expression is a mess of panic, relief, irritation, and maybe even fear, all tangled in the way his eyes lock onto mine.

"Did you just call me Eleanor?" I look up at him confused.

"I kept calling your name and you weren't answering." Noah quietly continues to assess me with the same expression.

"Oh, sorry I didn't hear you. But, there's good news," I say happily. "Hank figured out what's wrong. Bad news, he has to order a part, and it won't get here until at least tomorrow."

Noah finally shifts his attention to Hank, who launches into a technical rundown of everything the car needs.

I interrupt with a smile, trying not to treat the overnight delay as a disaster. "So, Hank, since it looks like we're staying the night—what's there to do around here?"

Hank sets a tool down and leans against the hood, studying me for a beat before glancing over at Noah.

"You lot up for a festival?"

CHAPTER 14

Even though it's a small-town festival, they don't hold back. Rows of colorful tents line one end of the fairground, each packed with local vendors selling handmade knick-knacks and tempting food. A petting zoo hums with laughter, carnival games flash and clang, and the air is thick with the buttery-sweet smell of kettle corn. I close my eyes and breathe it in—warm, nostalgic, alive.

Suddenly, whoops and hollers echo from a barn up ahead. I don't wait for the boys, just follow the noise.

Inside, the barn glows under strings of twinkling lights. In the far corner, a wooden stage creaks under a live band, the music bright and bouncy. The rest of the space is a blur of boots and twirls as dozens of people line dance in perfect rhythm. I stopped cold in the open doorway, completely mesmerized.

"I never understand how everyone just knows these," Ollie says, suddenly appearing beside me.

"It's like the Macarena. I don't remember learning it, you just... know it," I reply, grabbing his hand and tugging him toward the crowd. "Come on, let's dance."

He hesitates, glancing at the dancers with a half-smile. Then he shrugs and lets me pull him into the nearest line.

I catch Noah's eye and wave him over, but he only shakes his head, leaning against the barn wall like a moody statue. Classic party pooper.

I throw myself into the dance, stomping and spinning in time with the rhythm. Ollie, on the other hand, stomps at random and twirls when everyone else does. I laugh the entire way through.

We keep dancing through a few more songs. No one pays us any attention; everyone's too caught up in their own moves and friend groups, which is honestly perfect.

"See the girl in the cowgirl boots?" Ollie leans in, shouting over the music. "Should I ask her to dance?"

I arch an eyebrow. "You'll need to be more specific than that, Ol. Ninety percent of the girls in here are wearing cowgirl boots."

"Brown boots, denim skirt, blonde hair in curls. Keeps glancing over like she's some kind of siren trying to summon me. Specific enough?"

"Oh, the siren. Why didn't you just say so?" I deadpan, just as a slow song begins to play.

Ollie grins, nudges me with his elbow, then switches into his American drawl. "That's my cue." He tips the bill of his John Deere cap and heads toward the blonde.

I watch her nod, and soon they're swaying together on the dance floor. When I turn to Noah, he's still propped against the barn wall like he's personally holding it up. He had disappeared earlier but slipped right back to his spot.

Before I reach him, someone steps in front of me—a guy about my age, all charm and a belt buckle that looks heavier than he is. Surprisingly, no cowboy hat.

"Hey," he says with a smile. "Wanna dance?"

I smile back, about to answer, but before a word escapes, Noah's there. He gently but firmly takes my hand and guides me away from Mr. Belt Buckle. Once clear, he turns to face me and silently takes my other hand, the one resting on my waist, as we begin to sway.

He doesn't say anything, just moves with a casual ease that somehow still feels deliberate. He's not showy, just steady.

"Oh. So now you want to dance," I tease.

"Trust me, I did you a favor," he replies, nearly grumbling.

"Really? Why's that?"

"I rescued you from some overly eager guy in a John Deere hoodie."

"Right. Talk about a walking red flag," I say, fighting a smile. "Though maybe he's the prince of Denmark using John Deere as his American disguise. Like another prince we know. Ever think of that?"

"If that's his disguise, he needs a better one. We both know Ollie's disguise needs work."

I can't stop smiling—not just because I'm dancing with Noah, but because I didn't expect to be. If I'd known it only took another guy asking me to dance, I would've recruited someone the moment we walked into this barn.

"You're good at this," I say as he spins me out and pulls me back, his hand warm on my back. "I was starting to think maybe you didn't dance. Like you're from that town in *Footloose*."

Noah laughs, and I glance up to meet his eyes. The music slows, the lights dim slightly, and suddenly the air shifts around us.

His hand tightens slightly on my waist, and suddenly the crowd melts away. It's just us—electricity crackling between us strong enough to light the entire White House at Christmas, maybe all of DC.

I glance at his mouth, then back to his eyes. He tilts his head as if about to close the space between us, thinking the exact same thing I am. Just before he commits to it though he blinks and pulls back.

The song ends. I swallow my disappointment, trying not to show it. Ollie appears right on cue, slinging an arm around my shoulders.

"What do you two crazy kids say we grab some of that festival food?"

CHAPTER 15

As we step into the sunlight outside the barn, the low rumble of an engine pulls my attention to the neighboring field.

"Oh!" I point across the fairgrounds where a flatbed trailer, hitched to a tractor, is loading up. "A hayride. We have to go."

I break into a jog, but Ollie steps directly into my path, standing firm like a human barricade.

"Absolutely not," he says, arms crossed tight over his chest like a grumpy statue.

I turn back to face him. He's rooted in place, jaw tense.

"I am not sitting on something animals eat."

"That's the dumbest thing I've heard all day. We're going."

I pivot again and head toward the hayride line, but his voice catches me mid-stride.

"Elllllie," he whines, drawing out my name like a kid who's just been told recess is over. "I'm allergic."

I glance back at him, raising an eyebrow. "Since

when?"

"Since I was seven. My nanny took me to the stables to see the horses, and I ended up with hay fever."

I throw my head back and laugh. "That sentence was so pretentious. Nice try, though—hay fever isn't even caused by hay."

Spinning on my heel, I march back toward him, grab his wrist, and tug him forward. "Hayrides are in every cute TV show. I'm not missing out."

I'm not even sure why I want it so badly. Maybe it's the freedom in those teen dramas—the way the characters sit on hay bales under the stars, carefree, glowing, their whole lives ahead of them. I've watched enough of those shows to know the hayride isn't just background noise. It's a ritual. A moment. The kind of night where something changes—a first kiss, a secret told, the start of something big.

For me, it's just a hayride.

At least, that's what I keep telling myself.

And I'm definitely not looking at Noah as I say it.

Ollie groans, so I drop his hand, giving him an easy out.

"Fine, don't come. But you're seriously going to miss out."

Noah clears his throat. "We should stick together."

Ollie sighs like he's being asked to donate a kidney. "Okay, fine. But only if we get a caramel apple first."

I grin. "Deal."

While Ollie and Noah head off toward the food booths, I join the line for the hayride.

A group of teenagers stand ahead of me, laughing and bumping shoulders like they don't have a care in the world. They look like they stepped out of one of those coming-of-age shows—normal, effortlessly cool.

The kind of people who don't have security teams shadowing them or their face splashed across tabloids.

"Hey," a voice casually calls out.

A dark-haired guy turns to face me, flashing a confident grin. "Haven't seen you around before. Are you new to town?"

"Me? Oh, uh…" I stammer, caught in his green eyes as he runs a hand through his hair. He's tall, self-assured, and definitely aware of how attractive he is. Words completely fail me, which only makes his smile widen.

Get it together, Ellie. It's just a boy. A cute boy, sure, but—

He's not as cute as Noah.

My gaze shifts past him, scanning the crowd for Noah.

"You visiting?" he asks, mercifully breaking the silence.

I nod. His grin stretches further as he glances around, clearly enjoying the upper hand.

"You here by yourself?"

"No. With friends."

"Ah, she speaks," he teases, but there's no edge to it.

He steps in a little closer. "Did your friends ditch you?"

"No, they're just getting food." I motion toward the vendors, hoping Noah and Ollie are actually somewhere in that direction.

"Hmm." He follows my gaze, then looks back at me. "Better hold their spots then."

He grins again. But before I can decide if I even want to keep talking to him, his phone buzzes with an unfamiliar ringtone. He pulls it from his pocket to silence the call, and that's when I see it. A sticker on the back of his phone case.

Vote Kirkman.

The tiny buzz I felt from a cute guy flirting with me nosedives.

"You're a Kirkman supporter?" I nod toward the sticker representing my dad's opponent, keeping my voice as casual as I can manage.

"Oh yeah. Hastings is ruining the country. If he wins again, I'm moving to Canada or something."

I force a laugh, thin and hollow, the kind that tastes like nerves.

I don't want him to know who I really am—not because I care what he thinks, but because one simple moment could tip off security. And the last thing I need is to be dragged back home by a bodyguard in aviators and a grimace.

Still, it's hard not to launch into a full-blown political rant about why my dad deserves reelection more than

Kirkman. Man, the urge is strong.

"So," the boy says, sliding an arm around my shoulders like we're in some terrible teen drama. "Do I get to know your name?"

I look up at him and feel absolutely nothing. No spark, no butterflies, no cinematic music swelling in the background. Just the weight of his arm and the low hum of anxiety thrumming under my skin. This moment could sour fast.

Before I can answer—or even lie—he lets out a soft, surprised whimper and jerks his arm back.

I blink, then turn, and crash straight into Noah's chest.

He's gripping the boy's wrist, calm as a whisper but firm enough to hurt. His expression is neutral, controlled, but there's something dangerous simmering underneath. A warning in silence.

Noah's eyes turn dark as he stares the guy down. Without saying a word, he shifts his stance and steps in front of me, subtle but solid. A shield.

"Is there a reason you were touching her?" His voice is calm. Controlled. Deadly.

I blink, surprised by the razor edge in his tone. But I'm not scared. The guy is, though. He stiffens, backing off a few paces.

I reach out and touch Noah's arm, gently, trying to ground him. Ease him. He doesn't flinch, but he doesn't look at me either. His gaze stays locked on the boy, steady as steel.

"Uh... what did I miss?" Ollie appears at my side, holding two caramel apples, his expression a mix of confusion and concern.

Then, from somewhere in the gathering crowd, a voice rises:

"Eleanor? Is that Eleanor Hastings?"

And there it is.

So much for keeping a low profile.

"That's our cue to leave," Ollie mutters, tugging his baseball cap lower like it's a disguise and not a royal PR disaster waiting to happen.

"Noah, we've got to run, mate."

"I'm right behind you." Noah's eyes flick past the boy to the swelling crowd.

The Kirkman supporter is scanning faces, frowning. Confused. Then his gaze lands on me, and recognition hits. Yep. Time to bolt.

"You go left, I'll go right. Meet at the car. If we both run together, that's just another headline begging for a romantic subplot."

Ollie hesitates. I shoot him a look. "Count of three, got it?"

"No. Have you ever seen a scary movie? You never split up."

Before I can react, the Kirkman fan lifts his phone and points it straight at me. I freeze like a deer in the headlights.

Noah sees it too—and moves instantly.

In a blink, he tackles him.

I freeze as Noah slams to the ground, pinning the guy's wrists with fast, surgical precision.

"Go!" he yells, eyes locked on mine.

That jolts me. I bolt right, weaving through the crowd, legs burning.

I hear my name behind me—more than once—and panic claws at my throat.

I duck into the nearest white tent, lungs heaving, heart pounding against my ribs.

CHAPTER 16

Inside the tent, a woman draped in bright, mismatched scarves looks up over the rims of emerald-green glasses.

"Oh, sorry," I mumble, already stepping back toward the exit. But just as I push the tent flap open, I catch sight of one of the girls from earlier — the one who definitely recognized me. Even worse, her phone is out, aimed right at me. I can already picture it: me stumbling out of this tent like some off-duty Sasquatch caught on camera.

I let the flap fall shut and turn back around, trying to look like I belong. The woman is still watching, her expression impossible to read.

I force a small, awkward laugh. "Yeah, not weird at all," I mutter under my breath.

"I, uh… I like your scarves. They really, um," I glance around at her setup, "light things up." I wave vaguely at the crystal-covered table, cluttered with tarot cards, crystals, and, of course, a crystal ball. Her arms jingle with colored bracelets, and her light gray hair is tied back with—shocking—another scarf.

"Come. Sit." She motions to the chair across from her.

"Oh, that's okay. I don't have any money." I lean back slightly, checking if the coast is clear outside.

"For you, it's free. Trust me, this energy you've brought in has me curious. It'll be more for me than for you."

Her words give me pause. I hover a beat before slowly crossing the space and settling into the seat across from her.

"What do you mean? Is it bad energy?"

"Your aura's dark," she says softly, sympathy in her voice as she reaches across the table, hands hovering over mine. "Are you okay, honey?"

"What does a dark aura mean?" I slowly place my hands in hers, unsure if I'm just humoring her or genuinely curious if she can read my energy.

She glances toward the tent flap. Maybe she suspects I'm running from more than a phone-happy teenager.

Sliding a pair of glasses up the bridge of her nose, she studies my palms, tracing the lines with a polished nail that tickles lightly.

"See this line?" she says, following the top of my palm. "Your heart line—it's bright. But this island here? That signals heartbreak."

"Oh," I say, already feeling defeated. Great.

"Mmhmm," she murmurs, studying my right palm and quietly tracing the lines. "This is good." She gently places my hand back on the table. "You show signs of many talents and intelligence. If you don't already, you'll have a successful career and much wealth. Of course, wealth isn't always about money."

She reaches for the tarot deck and begins to shuffle.

Laying three cards face down, she says, "These represent your past, present, and future." One by one, she flips them, and I watch carefully.

"Knight of Cups." She taps the first card. "Knights are on a journey, right? This one represents yours. It's a journey of trial and error—learning through your experiences."

"Now, your present," she says, flipping the second card, "Three of Swords." Her expression softens. "There's been betrayal or disappointment in your life, hasn't there? A broken heart somewhere along the way?"

I bite back a laugh. "Heavy emphasis on disappointment," I mutter. Not necessarily right now— but yeah. Growing up wrapped in layers of protection, always watched, always guarded. No movies with just friends. No carefree teenage years. The only guys I've met were polished and pre-approved. Dull, dull, dull.

"It's not just about relationships," she continues. "You're holding onto the pain and sorrow. You're stuck cycling through it instead of healing. Take a step back. Ask yourself—what do those swords mean in your life? Letting go will hurt, but wounds do heal. Over time, your heart will mend."

She flips the final card. "The Magician," she says, eyes lighting up as I lean forward, not wanting to miss a word. "A wonderful card. It means you are the magician—you have the power to make your desires a reality. But... see how the card is upside down? That means you've forgotten your power. You'll need reminding—but it's always been within you."

"Like Dorothy and her ruby slippers," I think aloud, picturing Glinda's gentle smile as she tells Dorothy she could go home all along.

"Ellie?" a familiar voice calls from outside the tent.

I shoot to my feet. "I'm so sorry—I have to go. Thank you!"

She sandwiches my hand between both of hers. "You'll be alright, dear."

I offer a grateful smile before ducking through the flap. The sun blinds me for a moment, then strong arms wrap around me, pulling me close. I'm about to push away, but the sharp mix of sweat and citrus stops me.

"Noah?" I tilt my head up just as his grip tightens.

"Are you okay? Are you hurt?" His voice is sharp, but beneath it is pure relief. He pulls back just enough to scan me, then pulls me in again once he's sure I'm unharmed. "Where have you been?"

"I was getting my fortune told," I say, smiling up at him. "Apparently, heartbreak's coming, but it's okay— because I'm the magician. Oh! And destined for wealth." I hold up my palm and wiggle my fingers, knowing full well I'm twisting what she had told me.

But Noah doesn't share my grin. He's not smiling at all.

"You disappeared… to get your fortune told?" he repeats flatly, as if checking that he heard me right. He glances at the sky, inhales deeply, then exhales slowly.

"You told Ollie you'd meet at the car, Ellie. You can't just wander off, especially after being recognized. You're the First Daughter."

"Okay, okay." I pull out of his arms and start walking toward the parking lot. "Sorry, Dad."

Behind me, I hear an exhausted sigh.

"Ellie, I'm sorry." His voice is right behind me now. "You scared me, okay? I was scared."

That stops me.

"I was in there for like ten minutes."

"A lot can happen in ten minutes." His voice softens. "You disappeared this morning, too, at Hank's. Please don't do that again."

He closes the space between us, tucking a stray piece of hair behind my ear. Then, with urgency, he pulls me back into his arms. "Please," he whispers into my hair.

And I melt. Not out of guilt, but because this isn't protocol or duty. This is Noah. He cares, not as part of a job description, but because he genuinely does.

"I won't," I tell him, meaning every word. I can feel the tension he's been carrying ease at my reassurance. "I really am sorry. I went in there to hide, and then I just got caught up."

He slowly pulls back from the hug, and my arms drop from around him. People are starting to notice, whispering. But even amid the chaos, stares, and phones, I've never felt safer than I do right here, with Noah.

He silences something inside me that not even the best security detail could touch.

"Come on," he says, lacing his fingers through mine. I'm sure it's just to stop me from vanishing again—but I don't care.

"I told Ollie to wait at the car," he adds, shooting me a look. "He wasn't thrilled."

CHAPTER 17

We're at a park near Hank's shop and our motel. Ollie is playing soccer with a group of kids who can't be older than twelve, laughing as they race back and forth across the yellowing field. I sit beside Noah at a paint-chipped picnic table, but my eyes keep drifting toward the road. I'm expecting a parade of black SUVs to arrive any second.

Earlier, staying the night in this small town felt like an adventure. Now, with us spotted and photographed, and security likely closing in, it feels more like a ticking clock.

Noah finally breaks the silence. "So… you and Ollie?"

I glance at him. "What about us?"

"You seem close. And I remember that first night, you said he wasn't your boyfriend. But have you ever, you know...?"

I shake my head before he finishes. "Nope. Never. We basically skipped the acquaintances stage and went straight to best friends."

I smile at the memory—how we met at the inaugural

ball, the one where my mom dragged me over to meet the charming British prince. Ollie was every bit the royal cliché, but it wasn't until later, when he looked cornered by women twice his age on the dance floor, that I stepped in to rescue him. We ended up sprawled on the floor of an abandoned room, eating desserts we'd swiped from the kitchen and swapping phone numbers. He understood the spotlight when no one else did.

"My favorite thing about my dad being president is that it brought Ollie into my life."

A cheer erupts from the field as someone scores a goal.

"I sometimes fantasize about disappearing from everything, starting over with a new life, a new identity." I tug on the sleeves of my crewneck. "I tell myself I only have four more years of this intensity, but Ollie? He doesn't get a break, ever."

"You dream of disappearing, huh?" Noah teases. I can hear the smile in his voice, even though I'm focused on the makeshift soccer game. "What would your new identity be?"

"Jane. Like Jane Doe," I answer quickly, having thought this through before. "Just a nobody. Someone no one notices."

I keep my eyes on Ollie, who is now showing the kids some tricks. They act like David Beckham himself is on the field with them, but I feel Noah watching me.

"I hate to break it to you, Jane," he says softly, "but you'd never be someone no one cared about. You're not just the sunshine that lights up rooms and warms those who find themselves under your gaze. You're the entire sun. A gravitational pull that can't be resisted. The name you go by wouldn't change that."

I finally turned to look at him. His gaze is steady. I want his words etched on my skin so I never forget them—to have them tattooed somewhere on my soul. It's the nicest thing anyone's ever said to me—and it makes me feel like me, not a headline or someone's daughter.

My eyes sting with tears, and I hate how time with Noah feels like sand slipping through my fingers. I hate wanting to kiss him again, and I hate knowing it's going to end.

"Hey," he whispers, lightly brushing his thumb under my eye. "Why the tears?"

I sniff but don't pull away. "Nothing. Just… thanks."

"For what? Making you cry?"

I smile. "For everything. Not just being the getaway driver, but for making this feel like an actual adventure."

He smiles back, and for a moment I think he'll say more. Instead, he leans in and presses a soft kiss to my forehead—and suddenly, the electric current I missed with the boy earlier zips through every nerve.

"These kids are wearing me out," Ollie jogs over, panting. "I'm subbing one of you in."

Noah pulls back, his hand reluctantly falling from my cheek. "I'm on it."

As he jogs off, I turn dramatically to Ollie, feeling his gaze. "What?"

"Don't 'what' me," he says, eyes wide with suspicion. "Was I interrupting something?"

I groan, dropping my head onto the table. "Maybe? No? Ugh, I don't think so."

Sitting up, I look at him seriously. "Do you think this is like Stockholm syndrome? Or does that only happen if you're a literal captive?"

Ollie straddles the bench, brow raised. "Please tell me you're not comparing Noah to a captor."

"No! Just… hear me out. What if I don't actually like him? He's just the only guy around, and he 'rescued' us. Maybe I've been tricked by the proximity thing?"

He grins. "You mean that classic forced proximity trope?"

"Exactly! But isn't that just a romanticized version of Stockholm syndrome? I mean, I've known the guy for less than a week, and I'm crushing hard. That can't be normal!"

Ollie bursts out laughing. "Says the girl who locks eyes with someone across a room and starts mentally planning the wedding."

"I do not!" I protest, swatting him away.

"You do, but it's part of your charm. You're a romantic, Els. And you know what else is a thing? Holiday romances. Maybe skip the Stockholm syndrome idea and call this what it probably is—a fling."

I glance back at Noah, watching him pass the ball to a kid who scores a goal. He cheers, and I can't help smiling at the scene unfolding.

"I already hate that it's going to end." I admit, turning back to Ollie.

"Then don't waste what time you've got." Ollie wraps an arm around me in a tight side hug. "We both know it can end at any moment. I mean, maybe our security is lost and that's why we're still going, but, you know, don't take any time for granted."

"The thought of our security lost is both comforting and terrifying."

He laughs and knocks his shoulder against mine. "Love you, Ellie Belly."

"Love you more, Oliver Oil."

He leans in closer, voice soft. "Then take my advice. Go talk to him–*really* talk. Because Ellie…" he nudges his chin toward Noah. "You should see how he looks at you."

I raise an eyebrow as my gaze shifts between Noah on the field and Ollie next to me.

"How does he look at me?"

Ollie's grin is wide and knowing. "The same way you look at him."

CHAPTER 18

Dust swirls around us as we step onto a patchy stretch of grass behind a rundown diner. Ollie—ever the social butterfly—learned at lunch that a Lawn Mower derby is happening this afternoon. There's no way we can pass up on that.

I blink at the scene: grown adults wearing welding goggles and cutoff tees, revving souped-up riding lawn mowers with flames airbrushed down the sides.

"They're actually racing lawn mowers," Ollie says solemnly, pressing a hand to his chest. "I love America."

I grin but keep my eyes on the dirt track. "I don't think it's just in America. Who do we talk to about getting this into the next Summer Olympics?"

Noah laughs, looking around. "This is peak small-town energy. Honestly? I'm into it."

We watch a group of mowers line up at the starting line. The track's dirt, lined with hay bales. They're all wearing racing helmets, and even though I can't see their faces, I know they're locked in.

The referee waves a flag, and the engines roar to life,

coughing smoke as the racers inch forward.

"What's the prize for this?" I ask, squinting at the hand-scrawled poster on the judging table. "It says: '$100 cash, one bucket of loose fireworks, and a year's supply of bacon.'"

"Totally worth it," Ollie says, dead serious.

The flag drops, and chaos erupts.

Engines sputter, smoke billows, and one racer immediately veers into a hay bale. The crowd cheers like this really is the Olympics. A mower painted with sharp shark-like teeth zips past two competitors, the rider screaming something that sounds like 'FOR FREEDOM!'

We're laughing so hard, I have to clutch my side.

"Stop," I wheeze. "Is that guy drifting on a lawn mower?" I point toward a mower painted with orange flames.

"He's Tokyo Drifting a John Deere!" Ollie hollers, doubled over.

The racers barrel around the loop, one mower actually trailing fire, though no one seems even mildly concerned. A few blare their horns every time they take a corner. It's utter chaos.

Noah leans in, his voice just loud enough to cut through the noise. "You've got that look again."

"What look?"

"That 'I-can't-believe-this-is-happening' look."

I grin, breathless. "I don't think I've ever seen anything like this. Or laughed this hard in years."

"Then this race is a national treasure."

"More like an international incident," Ollie yells, pointing at a racer cutting through the concession stand. "That has to be cheating, right?"

The race ends in spectacular fashion when two racers collide just before the finish line, sending the bucket of fireworks—part of the winning prize—soaring into the air. They ignite mid-flight with a loud pop-pop-pop that echoes across the field.

No one panics. If anything, the crowd roars even louder.

"I hope no one was really counting on those fireworks," I mutter.

"You're going to tell your kids about this one day," Noah says, his eyes glittering as he watches the literal sparks fly.

"Only if they're very, very good."

The racers dismount, grinning for photos, while another group steps up to the starting line.

"People pay money for Formula 1 when this exists? Insane," Ollie says. "I need this broadcast on actual telly."

We stay put, watching the new lineup take their positions and placing bets on who's going to win next.

"Wait, look!" Ollie points to a nearby barn where lawn mowers rumble in and out. "Let's go. I have so many questions for those drivers. Racers? Mowers? What do they even call themselves? That's another question we have to ask."

Before I can protest, he grabs my hand and yanks me to my feet. Noah stands too, though the tightness in his jaw and narrowed eyes show he doesn't share Ollie's enthusiasm.

"Don't you think you could potentially be, you know… recognized?" Noah asks, his voice low but firm.

Ollie snatches the John Deere hat off his own head and starts tucking my red curls underneath it, twisting and shoving until they're mostly hidden.

"Ta-da!" He steps back with a flourish, presenting me like a prize at a county fair.

Noah raises an unimpressed eyebrow. "And you?"

Ollie runs a hand through his hair, tousling it in random directions. "Good thing I have an excellent American accent. Much better than someone's English attempt," he adds, nodding toward me like he's letting Noah in on a juicy secret.

"Yeah, still," Noah says, scanning the crowd. "I don't think it's a good idea. The fewer people who see you, the better. Besides, the next race is about to start."

"Too late, mate," Ollie brushes off Noah's warning and heads down the makeshift bleachers, which are just sanded wood.

I hesitate for half a second, but curiosity gets the better of me. I follow Ollie. "Come on, Noah!"

I jog after him, the cap too big on my head, forcing me to tilt it upward just to see where I'm going. Inside the barn, the air smells of oil, sawdust, and fresh grass. Racers fiddle with their lawnmowers like they're preparing for the Indy 500, not just glorified yard equipment. Ollie strides in like he owns the place—no surprise there. He's clearly not one to blend in, and it's honestly a miracle we've made it this far on our trip.

Ollie spots a cute blonde chatting with some older women and shoots me a look I know all too well.

"Don't," I mutter under my breath, though it's too late—he's already walking over to her, flipping on his twangy American accent. The girl giggles and tucks a strand of hair behind her ear.

Unbelievable.

I shake my head and glance behind me, expecting to catch Noah's unimpressed expression, but he's gone. I step outside for a moment and spot him chatting with an older man near the edge of the bleachers. There's something about the way Noah stands—rigid, tense—that makes my frown deepen, but I leave him to it for now.

I make my way back into the barn, letting my eyes wander over the mowers. One is painted hot pink, a perfect replica of Barbie's dream car; another one is decked out like the Batmobile. I crouch to admire the details of one that's been painted to look like Lightning McQueen from *Cars*—the detailing is oddly impressive.

"You like what you see?"

A deep voice pulls me from my thoughts. I jump and

spin around, only to find a boy—maybe my age—standing behind me. He's dark-haired, with striking green eyes that seem to size me up all at once. He's dressed in full motocross gear, like he took a wrong turn on his way to the X Games. The helmet tucked under his arm and the cocky smile on his face make it clear he knows exactly how he looks.

"Did you paint this?" I gesture towards the Lightning McQueen mower.

"If you like it, then yes. If not, then it's definitely not my lawn mower."

I raise an eyebrow. "And the correct answer between those two options is...?"

"I painted it," he admits with a grin. "You come to races often?"

"First one, actually."

He leans against his mower, sets his helmet down, and crosses his arms over his chest. "No kidding? What brings you here today, then? Heard there was a devastatingly handsome racer competing?" He winks, and while he's cute and friendly enough, it takes everything I have not to roll my eyes.

"Actually, yeah," I lean in, as if I'm about to tell him a secret. "That racer over there, number 43. Do you know him by chance?" I point toward a balding man who looks like he just stepped out of his shift as a fry cook at the rundown diner next door.

The boy laughs, then casually drapes an arm over my shoulders. "Trust me, I'm a way better use of your time."

I fake a gag, gripping his wrist to drop his arm from my shoulders. "Okay, Brad Pitt, dial it back. Does that line ever actually work for you? Because that was really bad."

His smirk morphs into a full-on grin. "You'd be surprised."

It's weird but nice. This guy is cute but I'm not nervous at all. Although I have a growing suspicion it's because of Noah. Because this guy is just...a *guy*.

Before either of us can say anything further, Ollie suddenly appears at my side, breathless, eyes wide. "Hey. Uh, I think the suits are here."

My stomach drops. "What?"

"I saw two guys—dark suits, earpieces. They're fanning out. I can't imagine an event like this would require security, so, you know, they're definitely here for us."

"Are you kidding me? They didn't find us when the car broke down, but now? Now they show up?"

I scan the room frantically for Noah, but he's still outside, and there's no time. My eyes dart around, searching for anything we can use to slip out unnoticed.

"Do you have anything I can borrow?" I ask the guy, voice tight with panic. "A helmet? A jacket? Anything?"

He's already in motion, grabbing a black helmet and a gray hoodie from a nearby table. "Are you okay?" His earlier smile is gone, replaced by genuine concern.

"Psychotic stalker ex," Ollie chimes in, voice flat. "What's a restraining order really, but for a piece of paper.

You know?"

"Please," I plead, urgency thick in my tone. "We just need to get out of here without being seen."

The boy nods and hands Ollie a white-and-black helmet before carefully slipping my black one over my head. It's heavy and awkward, making my head wobble slightly, but he steadies me with a hand on my shoulder. He then holds out the jacket. I slide my arms in, and he zips it up for me, fingers brushing my chin.

"Thanks," I say, genuinely moved. "Seriously."

An engine roars beside us.

Ollie sits astride the Lightning McQueen mower—and shouts, "Get on!"

"Are we seriously taking a racing lawn mower right now?"

"Wait!" The boy steps closer to us, eyes locked on Ollie. "I can't let you take this mower. I'm in the semi-finals."

I turn back to the boy, grabbing the edges of the helmet visor. "I'm *so* sorry! We don't have any more time. I promise I'll return all of this. What's your name?"

"Elllllllie," Ollie drags the name out, almost nervously, knowing the window for escape is closing in. I leap onto the back of the seat and wrap my arms around Ollie's waist. He doesn't hesitate, slamming the gas and jerking us forward.

"What's your name?" I repeat my question as Ollie moves us towards the exit.

He sighs with a shake of his head then smiles, clearly amused by the chaos. "Matt!"

Matt the Mower.

I file it away like a strange, vivid dream.

Behind us, someone yells as we tear out of the barn, dust and hay flying in our wake.

I pull the helmet visor down and tighten my grip around Ollie's waist.

CHAPTER 19

There's a race currently happening on the track, but somehow, we end up right in the middle of it. Referees wave red flags, and racers throw their hands up in frustration at our sudden presence.

Well, this is definitely not helping us blend in for an easy escape.

Ollie hoots as he passes one of the racers, enjoying himself way too much given the situation. Thankfully, when the track bends, he swerves between two hay bales marking the boundary and takes us off the track.

"Where's Noah?" I shout, twisting around to scan the wide-eyed crowd for him.

"I thought he was with you."

Ollie speeds out of the makeshift arena and down a deserted dirt road—surprisingly fast for a lawn mower. Guess that's why they race them. A black SUV pulls onto the road behind us. Yup. We definitely didn't blend in with that escape.

I tap Ollie nervously, mentally willing the mower to reach getaway speed. He glances back, eyes narrowing, then makes a sharp right into a field as the SUV closes in. I yelp as the mower lurches into a ditch, the rough ground scraping beneath us as we plow through corn stalks.

"I'm going to lift my foot off the gas, and we've gotta jump, got it?"

"WHAT?" I scream, heart racing. My arms instinctively tighten around him. "Are you out of your mind?"

"We're on a lawn mower! We're not going that fast. If we jump, we can disappear into the corn, and they'll keep following the mower."

Against all better judgment, the plan makes sense. I nod, adrenaline flooding my veins, the fear pushing me into motion.

Ollie grabs a hand around his waist and squeezes it. "Count of three," he says, already beginning the count.

At three, we jump. The ground hits hard, but adrenaline shoots through me, pushing me to my feet. We scramble into the corn, my hand still gripping Ollie's like a lifeline.

We crash through the stalks, breath ragged, until we reach a small clearing—an outer wall of a corn maze. I move toward the entrance, but Ollie tugs me back.

"No offense, Els, but we don't have time to solve that," he says, nodding toward the maze.

"Exactly," I reply, tugging him forward. "That's why it's the perfect place to hide."

A black SUV pulls into the maze parking lot, and my stomach drops—not in the butterflies-around-Noah way, but in the impending-doom way.

"Do we hide in the corn? We need to hide in the corn!" Ollie and I race to the maze wall.

"I'm sure they won't come in here," I say, my voice betraying more confidence than I feel. But that false sense of security dies quickly when I hear a buzz.

"Is that a drone?" I glance up, searching for it. Suddenly, Ollie yanks me into the corn, and I yelp.

He clamps a hand over my mouth and pulls me into a crouch.

"What if it detects heat?" he whispers, barely audible over the pounding of my heart.

The drone hovers for what feels like an eternity, but in reality, it's only a few minutes before it finally flies off.

"We're sitting ducks," I finally manage to whisper. "They know we're here. They'll bring more agents."

This is it. The end of the road. We might as well surrender. My breath catches, and I feel the weight of inevitability press down on me.

"This is whelmed," Ollie says, holding out a hand. "And this is me." He places his other hand higher.

I raise an eyebrow, the corners of my mouth twitching despite myself. "Overwhelmed?"

Before he can answer, a hand grabs my arm from behind. My heart leaps into my throat, and I yelp, flinging myself straight into Ollie's lap. We both go down with a thud, me thrashing to escape, his arms catching me by instinct.

There's a ninety percent chance it's security, and a ten percent chance it's an axe murderer. Either way, I hate my odds.

"It's me, it's me!" Noah's voice calls from the corn. He steps out, hands raised in mock surrender.

"Bloody hell, mate! Trying to kill us?" Ollie groans, still gripping my waist.

"I think your guys found you," Noah says, grinning despite the situation.

"Shush!" I leap over the spot where I've fallen on Ollie and slap a hand over Noah's mouth—never mind the fact that I just screamed.

"Oh no," Ollie groans, bending his arm to inspect the long scratch near his elbow, now bleeding. "Thanks, Els. You tackled me, and now I'm bleeding like a hawk."

I glance at Noah, and his confused look mirrors my own.

"Sorry, what?" Noah asks, visibly fighting a smile.

"That's not a saying," I giggle.

"Maybe not here."

"No, babe. Not anywhere."

Noah waits for my giggles to die down, which takes longer than I'd like to admit. Why is everything funnier when you're supposed to be quiet?

"Okay, so…" he continues, a bit more serious now, "what's the plan to get out of here? Because I don't know if you've noticed, but we're definitely surrounded."

"I don't know. I don't think we can," I say, the mood sobering fast.

"No way. We're not giving up." Ollie cranes his head upward, eyes scanning for the drone. "We'll wait until dark, then we dash through the corn and head back to the track."

"There's no way they won't be waiting at the car."

"Then we keep walking until we hit town and find someone who'll help us. Did that guy you were flirting with give you his address?"

Noah's sharp gaze cuts to me. "A guy?"

"Eh, it was nothing. He loaned me his stuff." I gesture to the helmet. Noah's eyes track down to the jacket, like he's just now noticing it.

"Right." He sounds... off, but I don't get why.

"Anyway," Noah says, "I drove the car here. It's in the lot. I tried to follow after I saw your little racing stunt."

This could work in our favor for a quicker getaway, but it could also be the final nail in the coffin. Surely by now, they have the details of the car we're in.

They're probably currently camped around the car.

Suddenly, a corn stalk snaps nearby. We freeze. The hairs on the back of my neck rise.

I want to grab Ollie's hand for comfort. I want to take Noah's hand, as if it's the last chance I'll ever have. But I don't move. I barely breathe.

"Couple spotted half a mile north of the abandoned mower," crackles a voice through a handheld radio.

My eyes widen as I glance at Ollie. A suited agent walks right past us—so close I could reach out and touch him.

"Ten-four," a familiar voice, one of my guards, responds before jogging off.

We don't move. I strain my ears for any other sounds—footsteps, voices—but all I hear is the pounding of my own heart.

"Okay, here's the plan," Noah whispers after a long stretch of silence. "I'll go first. Start the car, and then you follow in three minutes. Once you're in, we're gone."

As far as plans go, it's not great. But we're surrounded and out of options.

Ollie removes his helmet, then his cap, running a hand through his flattened hair. He hands the cap to Noah.

"Wear this. It's not much, but it'll help. Security's got a photo of you by now, so hopefully, it'll keep you undetected for a while."

Noah eyes the cap with mild skepticism. "I don't think this hat is providing the kind of disguise you think it does."

"Better than helmets," Ollie says, his voice flat. "They'll be looking for racers."

"Racers?" I raise an eyebrow at Ollie. "You get behind one racing lawn mower, and suddenly, you're a racer?"

"Hey," Ollie knocks his shoulder against mine, rustling a few corn stalks. "One race and I'm in the club. Besides, my mum would definitely have my head if I raced a real car. She'll be way more lenient about this."

Noah pulls on the John Deere hat, tugging it low. "What's the plan?"

"You don't get caught," Ollie replies. "You've got the keys. If you get caught, we've got no choice but to surrender."

Noah sighs and turns to me. "You good with this? It's a big risk."

"It's our only shot," I say. "Once they realize the lead they're chasing isn't us, we're done for."

Noah nods and drops into a squat. "Three minutes, that's it. You need to be there right after I start the car, so time it and then make a run for it."

"And if you're not at the car yet?" I ask, arching an eyebrow. "We're supposed to act casual?"

Noah shrugs, the tension in his shoulders relaxing slightly. "Okay, four minutes. The parking lot's not far. If you guys pop out and I'm not there yet, I'll start running for the car. No need for 'casual' at that point."

"Wait," Ollie interjects, grabbing Noah's forearm. "What if they start questioning you? Not arresting—just asking what you've seen?"

"No problem," Noah replies, voice calm but firm. "You popping out will be a distraction either way. We've got this window before they call in reinforcements."

Ollie nods, releasing his grip. "Right. Good luck, soldier."

Noah's mouth turns into a smile. He reaches out and squeezes my hand, his attention shifting fully to me. "Four minutes. Or three. I don't know—count, feel it out."

I squeeze back, a knot of tension tightening in my chest. This is about to come crashing down, but I'm not ready to let go of these moments with Noah. I'm not sure I'll ever feel ready to give them up.

"Be careful," I whisper, the weight of everything unspoken hanging between us.

"You too."

He stands slowly, his movements measured, the corn around us towering higher than our heads. For a moment, he can't see if any guards are nearby. Then he takes a few steps, vanishing fully into the thick of it, swallowed up by the maze of green.

Ollie and I mouth the count, but it's hard to focus on numbers when every sound feels like a threat. I strain to hear any hint of Noah's escape—shouts, sirens, murmurs, even the buzz of a drone—but there's nothing. Just the pounding of my own heart in my ears.

My chest is tight, racing like I've sprinted a hundred meters against Usain Bolt. My hands are shaking, and Ollie's grip tightens around mine—whether to steady me or simply to get me to stop trembling, I'm not sure.

At the three-minute mark, I take a deep breath, fighting the nausea rising in my stomach.

I close my eyes, sending up a silent prayer that Noah's hidden somewhere safe, engine running, while the world spins on unaware.

Three minutes. I inhale again, trying to keep the panic down.

"Ready?" Ollie's voice is barely a whisper.

I nod, rising to my feet.

"Wait." Ollie places his hands on either side of my helmet. "No matter what happens—whether this ends here or not—you're my best friend. There's no one else I'd rather be hiding in corn with."

If my adrenaline weren't so high right now, I'd probably cry at his words. They're a mirror of my own feelings. Grateful doesn't even come close to capturing how I feel about having Ollie in my life.

I lean forward, pressing my helmet gently against his. I don't say anything. My heart is hammering, and my stomach's lodged somewhere in my throat. Now isn't the time for words. Thankfully, Ollie gets it. He helps me slowly to my feet.

"Let's slowly cut through the corn in the maze, then, once we're in the clearing, we'll book it."

I nod, gripping his hand tightly. We move cautiously, carefully, following the path Noah seems to have taken through the corn. We don't speak, but my heartbeat is a constant boom—louder than anything else. It feels like some kind of marching band, and I can only pray it's not leading us to our doom.

We reach the clearing and abruptly stop. My helmet feels like a blindfold, and we both yank them off.

Ollie points toward the parking lot, and sure enough, Noah's in the car, engine running. A few SUVs and police cars are scattered around the lot, but no one seems to notice him.

I peek out further from the corn, my eyes darting across the opposite side of the lot. They're all searching in the wrong place, following the false lead. I wish I knew who sent them this false lead. I'd send them a gift basket. Because, without them, we wouldn't even have this chance to escape.

Ollie grabs my hand. "Let's do this."

With that, we step into the clearing and run.

CHAPTER 20

"Hey!" A voice shouts behind us. "Stop! You two, stop right there!"

A squeal escapes me before I can stop it. Being spotted sends a jolt of adrenaline through my body, like a live wire coursing through me. The moment of recognition sharpens everything.

Ollie's hand is still firmly in mine as we sprint like our lives depend on it, because, in a "we-don't-want-this-road-trip-to-end" kind of way, they do.

More voices rise behind us just as we hit the gravel of the parking lot.

"Don't even think about it, kids!" Marks—my head of security—shouts, but I don't risk a glance back. I don't want to know how close the trained professionals are getting.

Noah's already leaning across the front seat, trying to open the passenger door. Ollie, closest to it, jumps in just as I yank open the back door and dive inside. The second I'm in, Noah peels away, even before I manage to shut the door all the way.

"Buckle up," Noah instructs, his eyes flicking to mine in the rearview mirror. His voice is steady, but there's an edge of something deeper. The car accelerates.

Ollie and I obey without a word, both of us bracing for the inevitable string of black SUVs to appear in our wake. I'm not sure this car could outrun one of those lawn mowers, let alone the Secret Service, but we're going to try.

As if reading my mind, Noah makes a sharp left onto a new road. He follows that with a right, then another left, and another.

"Mate, do you actually know where you're going?" Ollie finally asks, breaking the silence.

"Hopefully somewhere they can't follow us," Noah mutters, glancing in the rearview as he takes another turn.

Up ahead, a barn comes into view, flanked by a giant stack of hay bales. Noah slows the car, pulling off the road and parking behind the hay tower.

"This should block the car from view if they come down this road," he explains, killing the engine.

"No way we just got away with that!" Ollie twists around to high-five me, and I gladly slap his hand.

Noah's grip tightens on the steering wheel. I know he's worried about the trouble he might be in, but he doesn't need to be. I'll do anything to make sure he walks away from this without a single mark on his record.

I think back to that feeling in the maze when I was so sure we were caught. It wasn't just the frustration of not finishing our trip—I couldn't stop thinking about Noah. How that might've been the last time I'd ever be around him. Ugh. Having a crush feels so middle school. I'm not about to start scribbling "Mrs. Noah Hart" in a diary, but he's definitely taking up more space in my head than is probably healthy.

Life would be easier if we could go back to the elementary school method and I slide him a note—check yes or no—to see if he likes me too.

And then, I wonder how hard it would be to convince my dad that Noah is harmless and should be allowed to stay in my life. Would Noah even want that?

"I'm going to check if anyone's home," Noah says, unbuckling his seatbelt and nodding toward a small rustic cabin. "The last thing we want is someone calling the cops." He steps out, then pokes his head back in. "Stay here, please. I'll be right back."

That works for me. I've done enough cardio for the day.

I unbuckle and sprawl across the backseat, closing my eyes in a half-hearted attempt to rest. But it's impossible—adrenaline is still coursing through my veins like I've been hooked up to a caffeine IV.

We sit in silence, watching a few horses gallop in the nearby paddock.

"Did you know there's competitive racing for those stick horses?" Ollie says out of the blue, his gaze still fixed on the horses.

A laugh bursts out of me. "There's no way."

"It's true, I swear!" Ollie insists, turning toward me with a wide grin. "I'll remind you to look it up once we're back online."

Oh, I will. But are these competitions for kids? For adults? How does someone win a stick horse race?

The driver's door opens again, and Noah pops his head back inside.

"Doesn't seem like anyone's here. I'm going to look around a bit more. If you get out, just stay close, yeah?"

Ollie doesn't need telling twice. He jumps out and heads straight for the horses.

Noah and I watch him go, a soft laugh escaping as one of the horses nuzzles him.

"He's not going to try to ride one, is he?" Noah asks.

"Nah," I assure him. "No saddle. And Ollie's not about to bareback ride a horse that isn't polo-trained."

Noah seems satisfied and heads toward an open barn.

"Find anything exciting?" I call, announcing my arrival a little while later.

Noah straightens from beside a wooden pen enclosed in wire. "Baby chickens," he says, pointing.

I hurry over, hands clutched over my heart, and peer inside. Tiny chicks peck at the dirt. I want to scoop them up and take them home.

"What? Oh, these? Yeah, just some baby chicks I stole on my road trip." I say, already practicing my casual introductions to my new pets.

Noah bumps my shoulder with his. "No farm animals at the White House?"

"I wish. Have you ever seen *Friends*? Joey and Chandler get a duck and a chick. That could be me. I'd take care of them."

He chuckles, glancing toward the field where Ollie's still with the horses. I keep my focus on Noah, though, drawn once more to the scar above his eyebrow—the one I noticed the first night.

"How'd you get this?" I ask, brushing my fingers gently over the scar before pulling my hand back.

"Would you believe me if I said I dove into traffic to save a puppy?"

"Oh, I assumed you rescued an old lady mid-mugging and then carried her groceries across the street."

"That's good too." He grins. "Better than what actually happened."

"Which was?"

He looks down, then back up with a self-deprecating smile.

"I was bullied as a kid."

The image of a younger Noah—sweet, wide-eyed, and too vulnerable—makes my chest ache. How could anyone bully him?

"One day at recess, a kid took one of the swings and slammed it right into my face." He points to the scar on his cheek. "Boom. Permanent reminder."

"A swing?" I frown, struggling to picture it.

"My dad picked me up from school and immediately signed me up for self-defense classes. I wasn't the only target—just one of many. But after a few weeks of training, I gave one of the bullies a bloody nose, and that was the end of it. There I was, a fourth grader, suspended for punching a sixth grader in the face."

I stare at him, wide-eyed. "They were sixth graders? And *you* got suspended? What happened to them?"

He shrugs, the flicker of a rueful smile crossing his face.

"Principal's office. That's about it. To be fair, I did break his nose."

He laughs softly at the memory, but something inside me softens, too. Noah doesn't open up about himself much, so when he does, it feels like a rare gift—like he's peeling back a layer just for me. And I want all the layers from the day he was born to this exact moment.

Why this job? How did he meet Sawyer and Leah? And why hasn't he called his grandma in California?

I reach out again, this time tracing the scar lightly with my fingertip. He inhales sharply, as though maybe—just maybe—he feels the same way I do. Maybe he thinks about that kiss at the football game as much as I do. I can't help wonder what it would be like to do it again?

His gaze drops to my mouth, then flicks up to meet my eyes… then back to my mouth. No one's around. No risk of security finding us. Ollie's still off communing with farm animals.

I lean toward Noah, pushing myself up on my toes. But as I close the distance between us, right before our lips meet, he rests his forehead against mine.

No.

He was looking at my mouth! I wasn't alone in this. I can't be alone in this!

I drop back onto my heels, heat creeping up my neck as the sting of rejection blooms. My cheeks flush—of course they do.

"We can't," he says softly.

"Can't or won't?" My voice comes out sharper than I intend.

"Can't," he replies simply. The flutter of hope I felt moments ago dies instantly. I imagine a kid, probably the same one who gave Noah that scar, grabbing the butterfly and crushing it in their hands.

Even though he says it simply, it doesn't feel simple.

"Because I'm the President's daughter?" I don't mean for it to come out like this, but my voice is sharp, laced with annoyance. Noah's gaze drops to the floor, and without a word, he confirms my suspicions.

I take a small step back, then another, trying to hide the hurt he's caused. It feels like a punch to the gut, a blow I didn't expect. Not kissing me because he doesn't want to is one thing. But not kissing me because my father is the leader of the country? That feels like a sharp prick to my facade—the one where I'm just any other girl. I'll never be Jane Doe. I'll always be Eleanor Hastings.

"Ellie," Noah reaches for my hand, but I jerk it out of his reach before he can take it.

"It's fine," I lie, forcing a smile so wide and polished it could win an award. Every inch of it feels fake, but years of media training make it easy to snap into place. "I understand. No need to explain."

But I don't understand. Not really.

I gesture over my shoulder. "I'm going to find Ollie."

I turn before he can respond. I think I hear him call my name, but I don't stop.

I can't let him see the tears that are already threatening to spill.

CHAPTER 21

I curl into the backseat, doing my best not to dwell on it. But Noah's rejection still stings. The way he pulled away, jaw tight, muttering that he can't. As if some invisible line is drawn that he refuses to cross.

Or worse: Maybe he doesn't want to.

I haven't spoken since, though I keep my eyes fixed on the passing landscape, hoping the miles will ease the ache. Ollie, however, hasn't stopped talking. He babbles from the front seat, completely unaware of the tension thickening the air.

"Ellie? Hello?"

I blink, snapping out of my thoughts. Ollie's waving a hand in front of my face.

"What?"

He squints at me, an eyebrow raised. "What's up with you?"

"Nothing. I'm fine."

He snorts, throwing a glance at Noah. "Never trust a woman when she says she's fine. She's never, ever fine."

Noah's eyes flick to mine in the rearview mirror, and my breath catches. I already know those deep brown eyes will haunt me for weeks, every time I close my own.

I turn away, pressing myself against the window, desperately trying not to feel— or show— how much it hurts. Maybe he's just overwhelmed. Sure, we did just outrun the actual Secret Service. But still… part of me really thought he felt the same way.

Before I can spiral any further, Ollie points at a passing license plate. "Wyoming!" He shouts it like he's won the lottery, and for a moment, the absurdity of it almost pulls me out of my head.

An hour later, Ollie calls his sister to check in. He chats with her for a few minutes, skimming over the whole "fugitive from the government" detail, and doesn't mention the memoir coming down the pipeline. I wonder if he's in denial, or just pretending it's not happening until our trip is over. Still, I catch the way he goes quiet sometimes, staring out the window, lost in thoughts I don't think I'll ever understand. I don't press him on it, though.

When he's done, he hands me the burner phone. "Your turn. Call home."

I eye the phone like it's a venomous snake ready to strike. "I'm not calling Grant."

"You're not calling Grant," he agrees. "You're calling your parents."

Hesitantly, I take the phone and dial. The phone barely rings once before Maggie picks up.

"Hey, Mags," I say casually, like I didn't spend the afternoon sprinting from federal agents.

"Eleanor, one moment," she replies, her voice all business. I hear rustling as she passes the phone, and I brace myself for my dad's voice.

But instead—

"Eleanor?" It's my mom. Her voice is tight with worry, and for the first time since we left, guilt floods me.

"Mom! Hey. I'm okay."

"Eleanor, honey, what on earth are you thinking? Evading security? And who is this boy with you? Do you even know him?"

"I'm sorry, Mom. Just call off the guards, and I promise I'll come home once we reach our destination."

"Which is?"

"Ha." I let out a fake laugh. "Nice try. But to answer your other question, you don't need to know his name. But he's wonderful. Trust me."

"Trust you? Eleanor, you've done nothing lately to make that easy."

I groan, feeling the weight of her words. "Mom, I'm safe. I swear." I take a deep breath, trying to steady myself. "How's Dad?"

There's a pause.

"Very interested in your whereabouts," my father's stern voice cuts through the line.

"Dad, look—"

"Eleanor Elizabeth," he interrupts, using my full name. "You ran off with Prince Oliver without protection. And today, you ran from your assigned agents? What are you thinking?"

"I said I'm fine. Ollie's fine too."

Ollie perks up at his name, turning toward me as if he wants to hear more.

"Let's keep it that way. You come home. Now. Before someone gets hurt. I mean it. Now, Eleanor."

"Oh no—I'm going through a tunnel!" I say, flattening my voice, then start making terrible static noises. "Tell Mom… love you… safe… gotta go—"

I hang up and drop the phone into the console like it's a ticking time bomb.

Ollie props himself up on one elbow and smirks. "Sounds like that went great."

"Yup." I pop the P for emphasis and let my head fall back with a groan. "I am so toast when I get home."

Before finding somewhere to stay for the night, we stop at a small diner. The parking lot is more crowded than I expected, and as we step inside, the smell of breakfast hits us instantly. Bacon, syrup, and a faint scent of something burnt fill the air. It's perfect—the kind of comfort we need right now.

We're crammed into a cracked red vinyl booth, Ollie practically vibrating as he pores over the pancake menu they serve all day, while Noah sits across from me, absentmindedly twirling his straw. I'm doing my best to avoid his gaze, pretending he isn't even there. Instead, I watch our waitress—probably not much younger than me, maybe twenty—and marvel at how she's juggling five tables and a busted order screen, her smile stretched thin like it's forced.

I can't help but wonder what her life's like. Almost as if my gaze has some kind of pressure, the top button of her blouse gives up entirely, popping off and skittering across the scuffed linoleum floor like it's trying to escape.

Her face turns crimson. She mutters a quick, "Be right back," to a table before practically bolting behind the counter.

Without thinking, I slide out of the booth and follow her. She's crouched by the swinging kitchen door, fumbling with the fabric, trying to hold it closed with one hand while desperately searching for a safety pin with the other.

"Hey," I say softly, crouching down beside her. "Mind if I help?"

She jumps slightly, startled for a moment by my sudden arrival, then blushes. "Oh, no, it's fine. Just… wardrobe malfunction of the century."

I smile gently. "Don't worry, I've had worse. Ever rip a ball gown on national television? Ten million people. Live. It's hard to come back from that."

Her eyes widen. "Wait… are you—?"

"Not right now, I'm not." I give her a secretive smile. "Right now, I'm just a girl who's really good at emergency fashion fixes."

She laughs nervously, letting me take the button for a second. I pull a small sewing kit from my pocket—Ollie always teases me about carrying it, but who's laughing now? After the ballgown incident, I made sure to always carry a small kit with me, especially at events like the one Ollie and I just fled from.

"Here." I thread the needle quickly, my hands moving on instinct. "Funny how often buttons betray you."

Within seconds, the blouse is patched up, neat and secure, like nothing ever happened. I smooth it down, and she exhales, relieved.

"Wow," she says, stunned. "You're, like… a magician."

As I stand, she looks at me like I'm more than just a customer, like I'm someone who sees her beneath all the noise. Like I might actually have a clue about who she is, like I've figured out the things she's trying to hide.

"Thanks," she says, voice quiet, almost reverent.

"No problem," I say. "Just don't tell anyone the First Daughter is out here doing pro bono tailoring."

She grins, and I crouch back down, feeling the weight of her gaze like it's a little more than I expected.

"Actually, this might be a really weird question, and I know you're super busy right now, but... what's it like working somewhere like this? Do you enjoy it? I mean, you get to meet all kinds of people. It's low stakes for the most part, though I *know* how hangry people can get. But really... what's it like?"

She gives me a look, as if I've completely lost it—and

maybe I have. "No, I can't say I enjoy it. But it pays the bills. I'm just trying to save up for college."

"That's wonderful! What do you want to study?"

"I'd love to go into marketing... but at this rate, a few more years of this job and I'll barely be able to afford one year of school."

I hold back a cringe. I've watched how hard she works, how much she pushes herself, and she's still not even close to affording college. It doesn't seem fair.

Before our conversation can continue, the chef leans out of the window connecting the kitchen to the counter.

"Let's go, Sidney. These pancakes aren't going to serve themselves," he says grumpily, directing his words toward us. I glance at the waitress and notice for the first time that her name tag reads Sidney.

"Sorry, I'll let you get back to it," I say, sliding back into the booth. Noah is watching me over the rim of his mug, and there's something new in his eyes—something softer, more uncertain.

"You fixed her shirt," he says quietly.

"No big deal. It was an easy fix."

"Still," he murmurs, his voice holding a note of appreciation. "You didn't have to."

"I know." I pick up my menu, my heart fluttering in a way I'm unwilling to examine. "But sometimes it's nice to be helpful in a way that has nothing to do with politics or protocol. Just… people."

Sidney arrives to take our order, and I slip back into my protective shell, pretending Noah isn't sitting across from me, feeling the weight of his gaze on me through the entire meal.

CHAPTER 22

Once we arrive at our rundown motel for the night, Noah quickly volunteers to run to the small shop in the lobby to grab some sodas. Honestly, it's the perfect excuse. Not only do I desperately need caffeine after the day we've had, but even more urgently, I need a moment away from Noah.

"Hey, so what's really going on?" Ollie asks as he slips off his shoes and throws himself on one of the beds, his gaze not leaving me.

"Nothing." I don't meet his eyes as I pretend to study the laminated TV channel guide, anything to avoid this conversation.

"I know that's not true. Come on, El, what is it?" His voice is soft, persistent, but there's a hint of concern underneath.

"Nothing," I repeat, more curt this time, but Ollie doesn't let it go.

"Ellie," he says, his tone gentle, like I'm a toddler caught with my hand in the cookie jar.

"Just drop it, Ollie," I snap, immediately regretting it. I

can feel my heart race, and I know I've just opened a door that's better left closed.

"Drop what? You've been weird and quiet ever since you disappeared with Noah. What happened?"

"Nothing," I repeat, the word leaving my mouth a little too quickly.

Ollie props himself up on his elbows, his gaze sharpening. "Ohhh. So *nothing* happened. Which means… You tried to make something happen."

Heat rushes to my cheeks. I spin around to face him, locking my eyes with a steely resolve. "Excuse me?"

His smirk falters, but just for a second. Too late. He reads the answer written all over my face.

"Oh my gosh. Ellie! You kissed him?"

I look away, gritting my teeth. "Can we not do this right now?"

"Oh no, Ellie Belly. We're doing this." He sits up straighter, then pauses, narrowing his eyes. "Wait. You're embarrassed. Which means—" His eyes widen dramatically. "He rejected you?"

"Shut up, Ollie." The tension thickens between us, crackling like the air before a storm.

"You're really mad," he observes, quieter now.

"You think?" I mutter.

He exhales, dragging a hand through his hair. "Okay, okay. I come in peace." He holds both hands up in mock surrender. "But come on, Els. If you're worried about the

'First Daughter' thing, remember—it's not forever. You'll get a normal life eventually."

I know I should let it go. I know exactly what he's really trying to say. But right now? Right now, I kind of want to fight. Because anger, at least, is easier to deal with than the humiliation swirling inside me.

"Oh, sure. Because no one has it harder than Prince Oliver."

"Come on, Els. You're in the spotlight because of your dad, yeah, but it's temporary. You go to events, smile for photos, shake a few hands, and then you get to go home. Don't want to go? No problem—as long as your dad's there. I don't get that luxury."

"Oh? A luxury? Really?" I can't mask the bite in my tone. I always thought Ollie understood what my life was like—that we shared something real, something that bonded us. But hearing him say this? It feels like betrayal. Maybe everything between us was just a lie.

"Well, yeah," Ollie says, rolling onto his stomach, reaching for the remote as if the conversation is already over.

Not a chance. I shoot him a look that clearly says, 'You're not getting away with this'. He sighs, reluctantly mutes the TV, and pauses on the guide channel.

"I skip an event, and it's a scandal. I don't get a vacation, Els. Once, I was bedridden with the plague," he says, giving me a pointed look. I roll my eyes, my smile barely there.

"Okay, fine, it was food poisoning. But still. I didn't

show up to some royal luncheon, and you'd think I'd declared war. My mum was there, but no, where's Prince Oliver? 'Why did he pull out?' 'Ultimate betrayal of the nation!'" He stares at the muted screen, his voice dropping.

"But you? You're not trapped. Not like me. You've got four years, maybe eight. I've had this since before I was born, and I'll have it until I die. And because I'm the heir, it's worse than what Sophie gets. The press doesn't just criticize—they humiliate me. And this memoir? It's going to destroy what little credibility I have left. I'm not just trapped, Ellie. I'm a punchline. I'm supposed to be this great leader, but no one will ever see me as more than some party prince."

"Don't act like the media hasn't dragged me, Ollie!" I narrow my eyes, my pulse quickening. His words sting more than I want to admit.

"For what? Your outfits? Your boyfriend's choices? That's not the same, and you know it."

"Boyfriend choices? According to the media, that's you!" I snap back, unable to hide the bitterness in my voice.

Just then, the lock to the front door clicks, and Noah walks in holding three cans of soda. "Who needs some caffeine?" He grins, but I don't feel like smiling. I push myself off the bed, the one next to Ollie's, and brush past him, heading toward the door.

"No thanks," I mutter, not sparing him a glance. "I need some air."

"There's plenty of air in here," Noah says, gesturing around the room.

I don't answer. I don't look at either of them as I storm out.

The hallway greets me with the sharp scent of bleach and stale carpet. My hands ball into fists at my sides, my breath shaky. Why does this feel like more than just a fight? Ollie and I never fight, not like this. Sure, we bicker about stupid things, like food or whether to call it soccer or football, but never about us. This is different. And it stings more than I want to admit.

I'm so mad at him. Mad at how he's brushing off my life like it's nothing compared to his. Mad at how misunderstood I feel. But mostly? I'm mad because he's right.

The media does love making a headline out of Ollie: Britain's favorite royal trainwreck. The British press is especially hard on their future king, almost like they're planting doubt in the public's mind about his ability to serve them. But that doesn't erase the suffocating weight I carry every day. They're both real—his pain and mine.

I head outside and sit at the pool, slipping off my shoes and putting my feet into the cold water. It's murky, probably unsafe, but I don't care. I haven't even been outside for five minutes before Noah shows up. He doesn't say anything as he takes off his shoes and sits next to me.

I don't say anything to him either. After the rejection of the kiss, the fight, and the endless chase from the Secret Service, I'm emotionally tapped out.

"Want to hear a joke?" Noah breaks the silence. His feet splash in the water, sending small ripples across the dark surface.

I don't look at him as I mumble, "sure"

"It's bad. Like, really bad. I mean, you're not even going to laugh."

"Then is it even a joke?"

"Yeah, just… an awful one."

I glance up at him, noticing the secretive smile playing at the corner of his lips as he watches me. I gesture for him to continue with his not-so-funny joke. He wiggles, sitting up straighter, clearing his throat before speaking.

"What did the horse say when it fell?" I keep my face neutral, shrugging in response. "Help! I've fallen and I can't giddyup!" Noah chuckles softly, and though I so badly don't want to laugh, it's just so bad that I can't help the smile that forms. Noah takes this as a victory, keeping his eyes on me.

"Why don't dinosaurs talk?"

I don't answer, just give him a questioning look.

"Because they're dead!"

I groan, and he beams, like this was his goal all along.

"Did you hear about the Italian chef who died? He pasta-way. Oh! And my roommate says I'm terrible with directions–so I packed up my stuff and right."

I can't help but laugh, covering my mouth. "These are awful!"

"I know, but they got you to smile." He leans over and gently wipes his thumb across my cheek, catching a tear I didn't even realize had fallen. "So, they worked."

I sniff and wipe my other cheek. "Thanks, Noah."

He hesitates. "Listen, Ollie wanted to come down, but I told him to give you space. I'll go if that means space from me too, I just... I wanted to check on you."

I stare at one of the pool lights, the way the water moves around it, making it look like it's dancing. I can feel Noah's gaze, though.

"It's been a long day," Noah says softly, like I'm a toddler who needs soothing. To be fair, though, coming down here was a bit childish. "You going to talk to him?"

"I should."

"I'll wait down here."

I start to stand, but he reaches across, his hand covering mine to stop me.

"Wait. Can we talk about earlier first?"

"Sure," I sigh, slumping back slightly. "You can be the first stop on my apology tour."

A flicker of something—hurt, annoyance, regret? — crosses his face but vanishes too quickly to identify.

"Apology?" His voice drops, uncertainty lacing his tone. "That's not what I—"

I stand abruptly, cutting him off. "Look, Noah, I'm sorry. I thought maybe… the moment felt…" I stumble, searching for the right words. Frustration bubbles up as I struggle to express myself without sounding completely foolish. "It won't happen again. Rest assured."

I give him a smile that I know is more pained than not, though I hope he's oblivious enough to it that it looks like I'm trying to pretend it never happened. I need to save myself from the embarrassment, to avoid the awkwardness.

I turn to leave, but Noah gently grabs my wrist, stopping me. I glance down at his hand on me, then back up at him, confused.

His eyes are wide, dilated—more black than brown—as the pool lights catch them. He pulls me closer, an arm snaking around my waist to keep me there.

"Today, I wanted to, Ellie," he says, his voice low, a mix of rough and soft. "You have no idea how badly. But we really shouldn't."

"Why not?" I match his tone, just as quiet.

"Because…" He trails off, like he's searching for reasons.

"Are you coming up with anything good?"

His gaze drifts to my mouth. "A few. But they're kind of getting tuned out right now."

His attention stays on my lips, and I can't help but lick them. Noah closes his eyes, taking a slow breath.

He closes the small gap between us, his mouth a whisper against mine. "I need you to walk away, Ellie, because I'm not strong enough to do it again."

I don't, of course. I can't.

Instead, I push myself up on my toes, closing the distance. Our lips meet, and the kiss is better than I remembered. My hands fist the front of his shirt, and his palms cradle my face.

The night is still, save for the low hum of an air conditioner.

How can someone I've just met mean so much so quickly? How can they hold the power to shatter my heart in such a short time? It seems insane, yet here we are. It doesn't make sense, but every inch of me feels it, the overwhelming pull of something I can't explain.

A car alarm blares, breaking the stillness. I jump, pulling away from Noah instinctively, but his arm stays firm around me, protective. We both glance around. The car alarm blares on for a few seconds before it stops, the owner oblivious as they pull a suitcase from their trunk.

Talk about bad timing.

I look back at Noah, his gaze already locked on mine. He gently runs his thumb across my bottom lip, the touch almost too tender. He brushes his fingers over my cheek, a silent comfort.

"You should talk to Ollie... It's important," he says, his voice calm but with an undertone of something deeper.

Even though I don't want to leave the warmth of his arms, I nod. He's right. Ollie is my best friend. And this, whatever it is with Noah, can't come before fixing what's broken between me and him.

CHAPTER 23

Noah stays behind in the lobby, handing me his room key before settling into a worn brown couch.

I take the stairs to the third floor, my heart hammering in my chest. Why am I so nervous? It's just Ollie!

But I don't even get the key near the lock before the door swings open. Ollie leans against it, keeping it ajar, his eyes wide with remorse.

"Do you hate me?"

I laugh, but there's no humor in it. He has no reason to apologize. I do. I notice Ollie's crestfallen expression, misinterpreting my reaction.

"No! Ollie, no, of course not!"

He visibly sighs, relief washing over him, and I gesture toward the room behind him.

"Am I allowed to grovel for your forgiveness?"

Instead of answering, Ollie grabs my shoulders and

pulls me into a bone-crushing hug. "You have no reason to apologize."

"Ol… can't... breathe." I gasp into his chest.

He quickly releases me, and we step into the room, the door slamming shut behind us.

"Yeah, so..." I tuck a piece of hair behind my ear. "I actually have a lot to apologize for."

"You don't—"

"Ollie, please," I cut in gently. "Let me just say what I need to say, okay?"

He gives a dramatic eye-roll, letting me know the apology isn't necessary, before going to sit on the edge of the bed.

"What you said was right. I'm sorry for how I reacted. I played the victim, but you actually have it worse. When my dad leaves the office, I won't be such a spectacle anymore. Sure, I'll always be watched, but like a reality TV star—nothing more than a curiosity. People won't care. But you? You're going to be king one day."

I start pacing, frustration bubbling. "You can't even get a Nando's in peace. Why is Prince Oliver eating Nando's? Why is Prince Oliver eating chicken? Doesn't he care about animals? Why didn't Prince Oliver order the Peri-Peri chicken?"

Ollie groans, rubbing his temple. "I'd kill for a Nando's right now."

I give him a look, and he smiles up at me. It's not the smile of someone who's trying to lighten the mood—it's more like the smile of someone who's resigned to the absurdity of it all.

"Hey, listen," Ollie says, leaning forward. "I belittled your feelings. Made it sound like my pain was more important than yours. That's not fair. Pain isn't a competition, and I'm truly sorry."

"Don't be. I get it. Sometimes, I feel so trapped that it seems like there's no way out. But at least I know there's an end. You're stuck until… well, until death."

"That's dark, Els."

"Sorry, but it's true."

He shrugs one shoulder. "You're not completely off the hook either. You'll still be in the spotlight, more than some reality TV star. Especially since you'll be spending most of your time visiting me. The media will always label you as 'former first daughter.'"

I raise an eyebrow. "Oh, I'm always going to be visiting you?"

He gives me a look that says, 'You know you will be.' "I don't care if our future spouses hate each other or if America and Great Britain go to war, you'll be visiting me. Probably at least once a month."

I laugh. "Oh sure, our countries are at war, the rest of the world is on fire, but here comes American Eleanor Hastings to visit King Oliver, yet again."

"Exactly," he grins, giving me that cheeky smile I've come to expect. "And if you don't come visit, I'll make sure our countries do go to war. The only explanation would be that you're being held hostage."

A loud burst of laughter escapes as I drop down next to Ollie on the bed. "Wow. You're going to make a great king. Your priorities are definitely in order."

"Seriously, though," he continues, his tone softening, "this friendship doesn't come with a time stamp. You're my platonic soulmate. You and me, we're for life, okay?"

My eyes well with tears, and Ollie immediately turned his body toward me, wrapping me in another hug.

"Woah, woah, woah," he says quickly, pulling back just a little. "I'm sorry! If you don't want to be friends forever, that's fine. You don't have to. I won't actually declare war!"

I let out a muffled laugh, my face pressed against his chest. "You're an idiot. But you're stuck with me, okay? You couldn't get rid of me even if you tried."

"Promise?"

I pull out of our hug and hold up my right pinky finger. Ollie grins, wrapping his pinky around mine. I swear, I have no idea what I did in this life—or a past one—to deserve a friend like him.

"Um," I say after a beat, "so… is now a good time to mention I just kissed Noah outside?"

Ollie jerks back, looking utterly stunned. "No wonder he wanted to follow you instead of me."

I whack his arm, and he laughs.

"I'm happy for you, and even happier that you're with

someone I actually like."

"We're not together!" I grimace. "In fact, maybe I should mention he, um, rejected me earlier at the barn."

"He what?" Ollie's voice rises in appalled disbelief.

"Yep. Something about my title—First Daughter of the United States, etcetera. Which might be why I was… uh, a little touchy earlier."

"But you just kissed? Just now?"

I nod, but before he can say anything else, there's a knock on the door. We freeze, our adrenaline kicking in. Instantly, we both think the Secret Service is here for us. I move silently across the floor, my footsteps careful, trying not to make a sound as I peer through the peephole. I immediately relax at the sight of Noah and open the door.

"Hi." I offer him a shy smile, which he returns.

"Hi."

A bed creaks behind us as Ollie throws himself across it in an exaggerated starfish formation, his hands behind his head as if he's settling in for a show.

"All good?" Noah asks, his gaze lingering on me. Those eyes are like melted chocolate—warm, deep, and tempting. It's like I'm Augustus Gloop, just waiting to dive in to a chocolate river at Willy Wonka's Chocolate Factory.

"All good," I reply, glancing over my shoulder as Ollie groans dramatically.

"I'm starving!"

There's no way he's starving; we only left the diner a couple of hours ago. I shake my head, a small smile tugging at my lips, then turn back to Noah, who's still watching me like I'm the only thing in the room.

"Sure, I could eat," I say.

CHAPTER 24

It's nearly midnight, and even though I judged Ollie for being hungry, I'm now starving in a way I didn't know was physically possible until this road trip. Not cute-hungry, not a little snacky. I'm talking full-on body-is-starting-to-eat-itself hungry. I didn't even know it was possible to get like this. At the White House, food is endless—meals, snacks, smoothies delivered on a tray, each with a lemon wedge and a napkin. No matter the time, there's always something plated like it belongs in a magazine. Out here in the real world? My options are peanut butter M&M's, warm Gatorade, and Uncrustables that have thawed and refrozen three times—because that's the kind of food you get when you're on the road.

Every street has been a dead end of dark gas stations or shuttered fast-food places until finally, *finally*, Noah turns off the highway and pulls into a cracked parking lot with one flickering streetlight and a glowing red sign that reads: Chicky's Cluck Shack. It's sketchy. The kind of sketchy that says, 'you might get food poisoning, but it'll be worth it.'

The drive-thru menu looms ahead, a massive backlit board plastered with greasy food fantasies and combo names that read like fever dreams: The Double Trouble Cluck-N-Bacon Explosion, The Cluckerfied Meltwich, Grease Goblin's Feast Pack, and something called the Cluck You Very Much. I can't even imagine what's inside these meals, and honestly, I'm afraid to ask. I know the head chef at the White House would die if he knew I ordered something called a Grease Goblin's Feast Pack.

Ollie scrambles upright in the backseat like a six-year-old on Christmas morning. "I want everything. I want to be buried in waffle fries."

"I just want something edible," Noah mutters, his face twisted with disdain as he squints at the menu like it's personally offended him.

I lean over the console to try to get a better view, my stomach growling so loudly it might as well be singing. Being buried in waffle fries honestly sounds like a peaceful end. A sharp crackle bursts from the speaker by the glowing menu, followed by a woman's voice so peppy it makes me suspicious.

"Hi there! Welcome to Chicky's, home of the Cluckin' Good Deals! What can I get started for you tonight?"

Noah glances over at me. "Ellie, you're up."

I sit up straighter, my eyes widening. "What?"

"You said you've never ordered drive-thru before," he says, smirking. "This is your moment."

Oh no. This is my moment.

He's right. Unfortunately, I've never done this. Not once. Not because I think I'm too good for it—it's just never come up. I went from being a teenager under lockdown to a young adult under… Secret Service lockdown. Food is always handled. Room service. Event catering. Security-vetted chefs.

Now I'm staring at a glowing sign filled with deep-fried choices and sauces with names like Ranchzilla and Sweet Heat Love Bomb, and my brain just can't handle it.

I leaned further over the center console, practically sprawled across Noah's lap in my panic. "Hi!" I yell into the intercom. "I'll take the Cluck You Very Much—wait, no, I mean, the Cluckin' Crunch. No, no, that's not right either—sorry, I didn't mean—"

Ollie's choking behind me, gasping for air between fits of laughter. He's slapping the seat like this is the greatest thing he's ever seen. Noah's shaking silently, head tilted back against the headrest.

I elbow him hard. "Help me."

The speaker crackles again, the worker's voice far too cheerful. "Take your time, sugar!"

I mutter under my breath, "You've given speeches to senators. You've negotiated in high-stakes meetings. You can order a chicken sandwich." My eyes dart back to the menu. Too many options. Too many puns. Why is this so complicated?

"Ma'am?" the voice calls again, still annoyingly patient.

"Yes! Sorry, I'll have the… spicy crispy Clucker. No— wait, the original. Not too spicy. Do you have, like, a medium spice? Never mind, it doesn't matter. No cheese.

Cheese on a chicken sandwich... is that normal? Is it better with cheese? Actually, yeah, just no cheese. Extra pickles? And um—what's a Cinna-Nugget? Is that... sweet or savory? That's not a chicken nugget covered in cinnamon, is it?"

"It's probably both sweet and savory," Ollie offers, sounding way too amused by this whole ordeal.

I feel my pulse spike. Okay, calm down. You can do this. "Uh, okay sure, yes to those. And just water. No—a Coke. Wait—can I have both? Is that allowed?" The words tumble out of me in a rushed, panicked mess.

There's a pause long enough that I start imagining myself bolting out of the car and running away.

"Would you like to make that a combo?"

"What's in a combo again?" I whisper, eyes flicking to Noah for guidance, as if he might know what would make me look less like an idiot.

Noah steps in, his hand brushing my lower back, grounding me as if I were about to short-circuit. "We'll take one spicy crispy Clucker combo, extra pickles, no tomato, fries, and a Coke. And a side of Cinna-Nuggets. Thank you."

"Anything else for y'all?" the speaker chirps.

Ollie shouts, "Four of your cluckiest tenders, large fries, and every sauce you've got!"

The speaker confirms, gives us the total, and tells us to pull forward. Noah does, rolling us into the glow of the pickup window.

I collapse back into my seat, heart still pounding.

"I blacked out, totally lost in the chaos. Did I even order? I think I just had a nervous breakdown in front of a teenage cashier."

"You didn't," Noah assures me, handing over some bills to the girl at the window, who looks like she's been awake for three days and fueled solely by chicken tenders and teen drama.

"Did I curse at the intercom?" I ask, half-serious. "Because I kinda feel like I did."

"Ellie, don't even worry about it. That was art. Pure panic art. I mean, frame it, put it in a museum. 'The Flailing of the First Daughter,'" Ollie adds unhelpfully. "Actually, let me think of something better. Something with chicken in it, probably."

"You did it, though," Noah says, passing me my Coke. "A complete rite of passage."

I take the drink with both hands, like it's a sacred object. The condensation rolls down my fingers, the cold biting just enough to remind me this is real. I raise it to my lips, take a long sip, and close my eyes. I can physically feel the fizz travel inside me, the way it burns a little in my throat before settling into my stomach.

"How's your coke-water?" Ollie teases.

"Okay, you know what, Oliver? It's a lot more pressure than it seems," I say sternly, though even I can't help but laugh.

Somewhere on a nearby street, someone is on their

horn. A dog barks in the distance. The smell of deep-fryer oil seeps into the upholstery. It's a scene far from glamorous, but it's real. Real enough to make me feel grounded, even if it isn't the escape I thought I was after.

I don't realize I'm smiling until Noah looks over and grins back.

"You survived," he says.

"Barely."

Noah hands me the bag of food. It's warm, heavy, and smells like every guilty pleasure I've ever denied myself. I open the brown paper bag and pull out a fry. Ollie's hand immediately snakes between the seats to steal one.

"Unbelievable," I mutter, lightly slapping his hand away. "You can't even wait three seconds?"

"Hey, I earned this," he argues. "I spiritually supported you through that meltdown."

"Did you already forget five seconds ago when you were calling it the 'Flailing of the First Daughter'?"

Ollie holds his hands up as Noah drives forward. "I said through the meltdown. Not after."

I toss a fry at Ollie's head as Noah pulls into a dark corner of the parking lot. The engine is off, but music hums quietly on the radio—some indie track in the background. We sit there, ripping into food like feral animals, dipping fries into questionable sauces, passing drinks back and forth as if we've never tasted different soda flavors. No plates, no napkins—just greasy fingers, too much salt, and laughter that makes your ribs hurt.

I take a bite of my sandwich—crispy, hot, definitely terrible for me—and it's the best thing I've eaten in months. Between that first bite and Ollie trying to explain what he thinks "Cinna-Nuggets" are supposed to be ("Like cinnamon toast crunch, but *bloated* cinnamon toast crunch."), it hits me: This is exactly what I've always wanted. And even though I can feel the embarrassment burning in my cheeks, I'm smiling because this—this dumb, messy, midnight moment—is real. Something unscripted. Something I'll never forget.

CHAPTER 25

The sun starts to rise, casting long shadows over the worn two-lane highway. The car hums softly as it glides down the empty road, golden light painting the landscape in soft hues of purple and pink. It's almost like stepping into a painting, and for a moment, that sense of freedom washes over me. The road is quiet—unremarkable, even—but the sunrise makes it feel like we're on the prettiest stretch of highway in America.

Ollie's already asleep in the backseat, his breathing steady and deep, and I lean my head against the window, a faint smile tugging at my lips. The hum of the engine is the only sound until Noah clears his throat, pulling me out of my reverie. I snap my attention to him, startled.

"How are you holding up?" Noah's voice is low, the kind of soft tone reserved for moments when someone's trying to keep it together. I consider his question for a moment, and for the first time in weeks, I find myself without a polished answer. Out here on the open road, there are no expectations, no political title looming over me like a shadow. I can actually focus on myself, on what

I want to do and say.

"I feel… different," I admit, my voice almost a reverent whisper. "I've spent so many years trapped in the political bubble, I forgot what it was like to breathe."

I glance at the side-view mirror, checking for any sign of black SUVs closing in on us. Okay, maybe I can't fully breathe. It's hard to truly relax when you're constantly looking over your shoulder, like some wanted fugitive.

"I didn't ask for all of this, you know?" The words slip out before I can stop them. "I didn't ask to be this symbol I've become. The perfect daughter. The country's future. It's suffocating sometimes."

Noah's hands tighten around the wheel, his gaze fixed firmly on the road. "I can't imagine. But you've survived it all, haven't you? You seem to handle it so well. I wouldn't have known you felt this trapped, this suffocated."

I meet his gaze briefly, a lump forming in my throat. "Yeah, I guess. But surviving isn't the same as living. I don't get to live my own life."

He nods, falling silent for a long moment. His thoughts seem miles away. The weight of my words hangs in the air between us. Then, his voice softens, almost tentative. "Is this what you wanted? This road trip, I mean. Just running away with no plans, no rules?"

I don't answer right away, instead taking a moment to think it over. Yes, I wanted an escape. I've been wanting one for a while. But in a way, I think it comes down to needing to feel like I can control something—anything.

"Was a road trip what I expected when Ollie and I bolted from that charity gala? No. I was just hoping for some time away from the weight of a dozen sets of eyes on me. But, to answer your question... I wouldn't say this is exactly what I wanted, but it's exactly what I needed. Does that make sense?"

Noah's eyes soften as he glances at me, and I'm suddenly aware of how close we are—not just physically in the car, but emotionally, too. From the start, I knew there was something about him (props to my instincts for sensing he wasn't a murderer after all). But over the past few days, it feels like something deeper has shifted between us. It's more than my insane crush; it's something real.

I like the way his presence feels next to mine—the way he asks for nothing, just simply exists. In my chaotic world, he has this ability to quiet all the noise around me.

"Yeah, it does make sense. I think that's the most important thing," Noah's voice softens, almost thoughtful. "You're choosing your own path, even if it's uncertain. Even if it's just a temporary path."

My heart does that dumb fluttering thing again, the one it always does around him, and I swallow hard against the lump in my throat. I shift in my seat, my fingers brushing against the cool fabric of the seatbelt as I turn to face him more fully.

"I don't know what's next," I say, my voice full of yearning, "I just know I don't want it to end. Not yet. This... this freedom." I glance out the window again, a mix of hope and fear tightening in my chest. "I'm scared it's going to be taken away any second."

Instinctively, my eyes drift back to the side mirror.

"Whatever happens next, you're not alone. You've got Ollie, and now you've got me."

I meet his eyes. My heart hammers in my chest. There's something in the way he looks at me—something unspoken, but unmistakably clear. Maybe it's the way he seems to know exactly who I am. Or maybe it's just the way he makes me feel like I can finally exist in this world, free from the weight of expectations.

I give him a small smile, one that is more genuine than any I've worn for the cameras. "Thank you," I say quietly, unsure if I'll ever say it enough. "For talking to me. For trusting two complete strangers who were about to steal— I mean, borrow," I add with a teasing smile, "your company's van."

I let out a laugh, despite the seriousness of our conversation. Just hearing how insane it all sounds out loud—Noah agreeing to take two people he'd briefly thought had stolen the Declaration of Independence on a road trip—all because he'd maxed out his PTO and his boss was forcing him to take some time off. He wanted an adventure. Twenty-somethings really do think they're invincible.

Noah's lips twitch upward, his eyes flickering with something almost tender before he turns his attention back to the road.

"Anytime, Ellie. Anytime."

CHAPTER 26

Noah dashed into the grocery store to grab some essentials that could stretch our shrinking funds—anything to help us avoid spending more on takeout. We all agreed it was probably best for Ollie and me to stay in the car while he ran in.

The windows were rolled down, the soft hum of the radio filling the quiet. I turn to face Ollie in the backseat.

"I've been thinking about college," I admit. "And what I might want to major in."

Ollie's sprawled across the entire backseat, his feet dangling out the open window. "What?"

I shift in my chair, reclining it all the way back. "Yeah, it's been on my mind a lot lately, especially during this trip. You know, trying to figure out what I'm supposed to do with my life."

"Els, that's great! Why don't you sound excited about it, though?"

"I can't decide what to actually major in," I reply, frustration creeping into my voice. "I have this fear I'll hate it and end up stuck, just feeling trapped in my own life."

"Okay, well, hit me with the top contenders." Ollie pulls his feet back into the car and sits up, giving me his full attention.

I drum my fingers on my thigh, thinking. "I could do Political Science. It makes sense, considering, you know..." I wave a hand vaguely, as if being the President's daughter is just some minor personality trait.

Ollie snorts. "I dunno, Els, maybe too obvious. What's next?"

I straighten up, feeling a flicker of determination. "Journalism."

"Breaking news: First Daughter Becomes Reporter, Calls Out Government Corruption." Ollie drops his voice to a low monotone, mimicking a newscaster. "Sounds like your dad's worst nightmare. You could always write about how great England and their prince are, though."

I roll my eyes. "It's a real option, though! I like writing, and I want to tell real stories, not just the polished political spin my parents' team puts out."

Ollie nods. "Alright, what else?"

I hesitate. "Fashion design."

His eyes widen. "What? That's not what I expected on my bingo card."

I laugh, a little self-conscious. "It's not a crazy idea. I love fashion. I spend half my time at state events mentally redesigning people's outfits—because, come on, Ollie, you know they're so dull! Plus, I already have a built-in platform. People analyze my outfits like it's their job."

"Because it *is* their job," Ollie points out. "At least for some of them. But okay, I'm into this. You could be like... the first First Daughter to win a Met Gala, instead of just attending one."

"Win the Met Gala? You do know that's not an award show, right?" I grin, feeling a little more confident. "I just... I don't know if it's serious enough. My whole life has been surrounded by serious people and politics. What if picking something creative makes me seem—"

"Normal?" Ollie finishes. "Els, you've spent your whole life being groomed for a future you didn't choose. Now you get to choose. So why not pick something that makes you happy?"

I bite my bottom lip, feeling the weight of his words. "You think fashion can make me happy?"

"I think you think it can," he says simply. "And I think you should stop worrying about what everyone else might say about it."

I exhale slowly, eyes drifting to the parking lot. For the first time, it feels like I have a chance to make a decision that's truly mine—one that isn't dictated by anyone else's expectations.

"I'm happy for you. This is a big step," Ollie adds with a grin, though his eyes linger a little too long, as if wondering if my decision will pull me further away from him. "But I still think we should make up a position for you on my staff, so we can hang out all the time. Fine,

fine—do what you want to do. I guess now you can design all my clothes. Imagine that—I'll have my very own personal designer!"

"Sure," I tease, leaning back. "Honestly, Ol, can you imagine my dad when I tell him? Maybe I should just stick with political science."

"Right, because political science is your dream," Ollie replies flatly. "Maybe you just need to practice how you'll tell them."

"Okay, yeah, good idea. You are my parents." I sit up, facing him.

"Hello, Eleanor, welcome to my office." Ollie drops into a deep American accent.

"Dad, I've been thinking, and I want to go to school for fashion design."

"Eleanor Hastings, as President of the United States, and more importantly, as your father, I must ask—have you lost your mind?"

I groan, dropping my head back. "Ollie."

"What?" He grins. "I just want you to be prepared for a worst-case scenario."

I look back at him, giving him a sharp glare. "Worst-case scenario? They send me to a remote diplomatic post in Antarctica, and I spend the rest of my life designing parkas."

He chuckles, shaking his head. "See? That's why we practice." He nudges my shoulder lightly, his usual smirk returning. "Alright, let's try again. Hit me with your opening statement."

I inhale deeply, square my shoulders, and clasp my hands together like I'm about to address Congress. "Mom, Dad, I've decided on my major. I'm going to study fashion design."

Ollie gasps dramatically, slapping a hand over his heart as though I've just announced the apocalypse. "Fashion? But Eleanor, what will people say?" He throws his arms out wide, barely containing a smirk. "The headlines! 'First Daughter Abandons Politics for Parisian Runways!' Or—oh, 'First Daughter Becomes Private Royal Designer!'"

I roll my eyes, exasperated. "Okay, seriously, that's not helping."

He raises his hands in surrender. "Fine, fine," he says, waving them dismissively. "Let's make it stronger. Lead with something they can't argue with."

I take another deep breath. "I want to make a difference in the world, and fashion is how I plan to do it."

Ollie raises an eyebrow, clearly unconvinced. "Nice. Now, back that up."

I nod, determination settling in. "Fashion is more than just clothes—it's communication. It's power. It's how people present themselves to the world. Think about how much attention gets paid to what Mom or I wear to state dinners, or what you, Dad, wear during debates. People analyze every detail."

Ollie nods, clearly following my reasoning, but I can see the skepticism in his eyes. "Good, good. Now, connect it to you.”

I hesitate, feeling the weight of his words. What’s it really about for me? I close my eyes for a brief second before continuing. “My whole life, I’ve been expected to fit a certain image. But I want to be the one defining it. I don’t just want to wear the dress—I want to design it.”

Ollie’s eyes light up, a grin tugging at the corner of his mouth. “Boom. There it is. That’s the speech.”

I let out a long breath, feeling a sense of relief, but also a flicker of doubt. “You really think it’ll work? You’re not just saying that?”

“Well…” He taps his fingers on his chin, pretending to think. “No, they’re definitely going to freak out at first.”

I groan, louder than before. “Ollie.”

“But!” He grins, leaning in. “They love you. All you have to do is convince them that this isn’t just a phase— it’s what’ll make you happy.”

I bite my lip. “And if they don’t listen?”

“Then remind them you’re a legal adult. And if they push too hard, well, you’ll move to Paris, dye your hair pink, and start couch surfing your way to the top.”

I snort, trying not to laugh. “Oh, sure. That’ll go over well with the Secret Service.”

“Perfect,” he says, “because instead of Paris, you’ll obviously run away to London.”

“Obviously.” I shake my head with a laugh, the tension in my chest easing, even if just for a moment.

Just then, Noah arrives, his cart loaded with mostly junk food. He dumps the bags of food into the backseat next to Ollie, who's already tearing into a bag of candy.

"Nice work, mate. You got a good haul." Ollie grins, picking up a piece of candy and tossing it into his mouth. "Mmm," he closes his eyes dramatically as he chews. "It's like I can taste the Red Dye 40."

"No objections if we take a quick detour?" Noah slides into the driver's seat with a playful grin. "I've got a little surprise." He looks at me briefly, his smile almost mischievous, before shifting the car into drive.

CHAPTER 27

We pull up to a barn, its walls glowing with strings of yellow twinkling lights.

"Oh! Is the surprise line dancing lessons?" Ollie leans forward between the two seats, his voice playful.

"A barn doesn't automatically mean line dancing, Ollie," I laugh, glancing over at Noah. "What is the surprise, though? It doesn't even look like anyone's here."

Noah smiles as he steps out of the car, leaning back inside with a grin. "You don't have to come, but you'll regret it if you don't." His smile is secretive, teasing, and I feel the pull to follow. Without a second thought, I unbuckle my seatbelt.

We walk past the barn, heading towards a nearby field where a man stands beside a tractor.

"Whoa, that guy looks like Santa," Ollie murmurs, his tone low as he watches Noah shake the man's hand.

They exchange words for a moment while Ollie and I exchange a few confused glances. Noah turns towards us, motioning for us to come over.

"Frank, this is Jane and Robby." I stifle a smile at the names—our perfect aliases. "Guys, this is Frank." He introduces us, and sure enough, Ollie was right. The man looks like Santa, only dressed in denim.

After a brief conversation, Noah leads me toward the back of the tractor, where a flatbed trailer is hitched. He holds out his hand with a smirk. "M'lady, your chariot awaits."

I raise an eyebrow, but a smile tugs at the corner of my lips as I take his hand. His touch is warm, a stark contrast to the crisp chill in the air. He helps me up onto the hay-covered trailer, and the rough edges jab through my jeans as I settle into the makeshift seat. The whole scene smells like earth, autumn, and something faintly sweet—maybe the apple orchard we passed on the drive here.

As I sit there, I scan my surroundings, still trying to make sense of whether this is really happening. The sky is a deep indigo, dotted with faint stars. The kind you never get in DC.

"What exactly is happening right now?" I ask, my voice low as I watch Ollie, still deep in conversation with Frank. Frank nods, listening intently as he climbs into the tractor. Ollie follows, his silhouette animated, bouncing with enthusiasm as he climbs into the driver's seat. The engine rumbles to life, and the trailer jolts beneath me.

"You're getting your hayride," Noah says beside me, his voice casual, like this is a totally normal Friday night plan.

I turn toward him. "You did this?"

He shrugs, as if it's no big deal. "I felt bad you didn't get to experience a hayride like the ones on TV. You were pretty excited about it back at the festival."

"You remember that? I mentioned it once."

"Once, with the enthusiasm of a child on Christmas Eve." He leans in slightly, his shoulder brushing mine. "It was nothing. I just looked up some local farms, made a few calls, and asked if anyone would help make someone's dream come true."

His voice softens as he adds, "But if anyone asks, you're suffering from a rare disease called première fille."

I laugh despite myself, fighting the urge to swoon like some rom-com heroine. "Okay, and what exactly is that?"

He flashes a crooked, conspiratorial smile. "It's First Daughter in French."

"Ah, yes. Tragic," I say, pressing a hand to my chest. "Suffering from première fille, indeed. Symptoms include diplomatic trauma and a complete inability to order at a drive-thru without embarrassing myself."

"Don't forget spontaneous hayride cravings and needing to be reminded that you're allowed to have fun."

That last part lingers between us—not heavy, but real. I glance down at my boots, then back to the horizon as the tractor rolls forward. The trailer creaks beneath us, hay rustling with each bump and turn as we pull away from the barn. The twinkle lights strung along the barn roofline cast a soft, golden glow, painting the night in warmth as we roll away. I close my eyes for a moment and let the breeze sweep across my face. Somewhere out there, a few crickets chirp. It's not the sound of power, pressure, or responsibility that I'm used to. It's just night—quiet, serene. A world of possibility I've barely dared to dream about.

This isn't a TV drama, but somehow, it feels like one. Except it's better. Because it's mine. I'm not on anyone else's schedule. I'm not playing a role in someone else's story. This is mine—raw and real. And it's all because of the boy sitting next to me.

It's probably cheesy to be this happy on a hayride, but I don't care. When I open my eyes again, I glance sideways and catch Noah already watching me.

"What?" I ask, my smile tugging wider before he even answers.

He leans a little closer, his voice low and warm. "I was just thinking… I've seen a lot of versions of you on this trip."

"Oh yeah?" I nudge him lightly with my shoulder. "Which version is this? Girl-on-hay?"

He laughs softly under his breath, then reaches up to tuck a stray strand of hair behind my ear. It's so gentle, it makes something flip inside my chest. "No. Happy. Totally unguarded. Where your whole face lights up just because you're exactly where you want to be, it's my favorite version."

I forgot how to speak for a second. The way he says it—it's not performative. He's not trying to charm me. He's just saying what he sees, and what he sees is me.

"I think it's my favorite too," I say, quieter than I mean

to. "I feel so… normal." It's like I've stepped outside of all the versions of myself I've had to hide. Here, with him, I'm just…me.

He smiles like I've just told him something important, like it actually matters.

The trailer bumps slightly as we hit a rut in the dirt path. I shift to face him more fully, tucking one leg beneath me.

"You know, I can't help but wonder," he says after a beat, "what even is normal, anyway? Who decided that?"

I let the question linger between us for a moment. "I guess... normal is walking down a street and not being recognized," I say. "Not having your life decided for you before you even know what you want."

"Okay," he says, nodding slowly, "but what if it's a street in, like, Iceland? Or some tiny town in the middle of nowhere, one that's never even heard of the American president's family?"

I grin. "You think Iceland doesn't know who we are?"

"Maybe, but only if they're interested in the president and his family, the way some Americans are obsessively invested in Ollie's family."

I laugh, then shake my head. "So, you're saying I could go off-grid and live anonymously in a fishing village?"

"Easily." He raises an eyebrow. "You could totally reinvent yourself—change your name, live in disguise as a small-town scarf designer."

I stare at him. "Scarf designer? That's your go-to fake identity for me?"

"It's oddly specific, yes," he says with pride. "But hear me out. You'd be perfect with that cottage-core vibe. Picture it: You'd host scarf-weaving workshops in your rustic barn. You'd become a local legend."

"I'd obviously have to host line dancing lessons if I had a barn—because clearly, according to Ollie, barn equals line dancing."

Noah and I share a look, matching smiles, a crinkle at the corner of his eyes. Then, as if it's the most natural thing in the world, I lean in.

Noah doesn't hesitate. He meets me halfway. When our lips touch, it's warm, careful, and impossibly sure. It's not showy. Not rushed. It's just right. His hand brushes my jaw, and I grab the edge of his jacket, as if I might float away if I don't hold on.

It's not my first kiss.

It's not even my first kiss with Noah.

But it's the first one that feels like more than a kiss.

It feels like a doorway opening to something new, terrifying, and completely good.

When we finally pull apart, I'm breathless—in the best way. My heart's racing, like I've just sprinted the length of the National Mall, and I don't even care.

Noah keeps his forehead against mine. Neither of us speaks for a moment. We don't need to. Because this— *this*—is what it feels like to be exactly where I'm meant to be.

Not on a stage. Not in a spotlight. Not standing behind

a podium.

But here. On a hayride, in the middle of nowhere, wrapped in flannel and starlight. With a boy who looks at me like I'm not the First Daughter. I'm just me.

CHAPTER 28

Look! A shooting star! Make a wish." I point to a passing light in the night sky.

Noah squints, focusing, then glances back at me with a small smile. "That's definitely an airplane."

"Shh, let me have this."

Noah and I are sitting on the hood of the car, passing a bag of gummy worms back and forth under a sky so full of stars, it almost feels fake. Ollie paces behind us, talking to his little sister on the phone—the safest choice he had for checking in without getting yelled at.

Noah bumps his shoulder into mine, just lightly. "You're getting better at this 'being normal in public' thing."

I let out a short laugh. "Was that before or after I panic-ordered a Cluck You Very Much into the drive-thru speaker?"

He grins, clearly amused. "That was a highlight of the trip for me, actually."

"I blacked out," I say, laughing. "Completely blacked out!"

"You ordered everything and nothing at the same time."

"I was under pressure!" I defend myself with a playful grin.

He chuckles, leaning back on his elbows, a relaxed smile tugging at the corner of his mouth.

I glance up at the sky, still smiling, unable to stop. It feels good to let go.

I chew on my bottom lip, the smile fading as my curiosity takes over. "So, what's your story? Why do you want to go visit your grandma, especially since it seems like you're not exactly close with her?"

Noah falls silent, and a tight knot of anxiety twists in my stomach. I worry I've crossed a line, pushed too far.

Finally, he speaks, his voice quieter than before. "My dad is actually dead."

His attention is fixed on the night sky, and I reach over, placing my hand on his. His gaze stays trained on the stars, and I wonder if he sees anything up there besides just the stars. Does a sky full of them bring him any closer to his dad? Does it give him some sense of connection? I don't say anything. I'm not sure what to say. "Sorry for your loss" is probably a phrase he's heard too many times. I'm not even sure how much comfort those words offer anyone grieving. Instead, I just hold his hand, rubbing small circles on his skin with the pad of my thumb.

"My mom left when I was two," he says, his voice barely above a whisper. "She said she couldn't be a mother and was destined for Broadway, so she just left. It was just my dad and me for years. He never dated anyone else. We moved to DC for his job, which kept him too busy for much of a social life, but he always made sure to have time for me."

Noah finally looks at me, and I see the sadness in his eyes—the kind he works so hard to mask during the day. What is it about late-night conversations that makes you want to open up and be completely vulnerable?

"My grandma is actually my mom's mom. With my mom out of the picture, and my dad and I all the way across the country, we just... lost touch. I've thought about reaching out for years now, especially since she's the only family I've got left. But every time I try to, I get stuck in my head. Like, if my mom didn't want me, why would her mom?"

I scoot closer to Noah, my head finding its place on his shoulder. His words hit harder than I expected, and I feel a sharp pang of sympathy. "Of course she'd want to see you," I say, my voice soft but firm, genuinely surprised he thinks anyone wouldn't want him in their life. "The man you are today—your kindness, your strength, all of it—says everything about who your dad was. No doubt, he'd be so proud of you, Noah. As for your mom... honestly, it's her loss. She's the one missing out, not you. You're worth knowing, and I feel so lucky that it was you who jumped in that day to drive the van. I can't even imagine what it would have been like if it were anyone else."

Noah chuckles, tilting his head so it rests on top of mine, which is still nestled against his shoulder. "Yeah, well, when two well-dressed people are about to take off with your catering van, the adrenaline sort of kicks in. But thanks, Ellie. I'm glad it was me that day, and that I talked you into letting me come on this trip."

He reaches his right hand across, twirling a strand of my hair around his fingers before letting it fall. His palm gently cups my cheek, and he pulls his left hand free from beneath mine to hold the other side of my face. He's so pretty it almost hurts. If he'd been around during Michelangelo's time, there's no way he wouldn't have been a muse for one of those statues.

"I thought for, like, two minutes you might be a murderer," I say lightly, even though my breath catches, tripping over itself.

"Two minutes? That's it? Did you miss Stranger Danger Day at school?" His lips curl into a smile, and I can't help but want to kiss them. His eyes flicker to my mouth, like he's thinking the same thing, and I try to lean in closer, caught in his grip.

"You're so beautiful," he murmurs, his gaze tracing my face as though he's trying to commit it to memory.

"Do you think we'll see each other when we're back in DC?" The question has been haunting me. His answer terrifies me. What if he says no? What if he doesn't want to? What if he has a girlfriend back home, and I've become the other woman? No, I'm getting ahead of myself. Noah doesn't seem like the kind of guy who would do something like that.

"I'm not sure," he replies, and thankfully, it's not a definite no, but it's not a yes either. "I'd like to, though."

Just like that, his words spark a Fourth of July fireworks display in my chest. He wants to, and I want nothing more than that.

"Me too." I whisper, my mouth hovering over his. "I'd really like to, too."

CHAPTER 29

The next morning, I woke to the soft hum of a voice outside the motel room. The sky's still dark, the kind of early morning that feels like it's stuck in indecision, still deciding whether it wants to actually be morning or not. A chill cuts through the thin walls, seeping into my skin and nudging me awake more than I'd like. For a moment, I just lie there, blinking at the ceiling, trying to remember where we are. Colorado, I think. Small town. Tiny diner across the street— surprisingly decent pancakes. A world away from DC, and I'm still getting used to the quiet.

I pull Noah's hoodie on—it somehow ended up folded at the foot of the bed—and pad silently to the window, the floor cool against my feet. I push the curtain just enough to peek through, and there he is: Ollie.

He's sitting on the curb outside, phone pressed to his ear, back hunched like he's trying to fold himself in half. His breath fogs into the air with each exhale, though he doesn't seem to notice—or maybe he just doesn't care about the cold. His voice is low, muffled by the window and wall, but it carries just enough for me to catch a few words.

I glance back at the bed where Noah still sleeps, his arm flung over his eyes, breathing rhythmic and steady. I hesitate for a second, torn between crawling back under the covers and checking on my best friend. But the curve of Ollie's shoulders—tension wound tight—wins me over.

The door creaks, just loud enough to make me cringe, but I ignore it. Cold air spills into the room as I step outside, letting the door click shut behind me. The concrete is freezing beneath my bare feet, but I make my way over to Ollie as quietly as I can, and sit down beside him. I keep a little distance, not wanting to interrupt his call, but I can feel his tension, thick in the air between us.

"I know, yes. I saw it. Page twelve was especially creative," Ollie murmurs, the humor in his voice forced, brittle.

A pause.

"So that's it, then? You're all just… carrying on?"

I stare at the empty street before us. The parking lot is dimly lit by the flickering motel sign. A few moths buzz near the bulb, as if even they aren't fully committed to waking up yet.

"No, I'm not asking for a press statement or a royal rebuttal," He says, keeping his voice steady. "I just thought maybe someone else would be… rattled. Just a little, even."

His voice cracks slightly at the end. Not enough for someone on the other end of the phone to catch, but I hear it.

Silence. Then a soft laugh—dry, fake.

"Of course. 'Stiff upper lip.' Right."

Another pause. Another deep sigh.

"Tell Mum I'm fine and I'll be home soon… well, soonish."

He ends the call and doesn't move. The burner phone dangles from his fingers, its screen glowing faintly before dimming. He tilts his head back, eyes drifting toward the faint stars that are just beginning to fade into the early morning light.

I don't say anything at first. The silence is soft, like fog settling in, and I don't want to break it just yet.

Finally, he speaks. "They're not panicking."

"That's good. Isn't it?" I ask, trying to read his face.

He scoffs, but not unkindly—more like someone who's seen this all before. "Yeah, maybe."

I glance at him sideways. He's wearing that faraway look again, the one he gets when thoughts of home, duty, and whatever crown-shaped weight he's carrying drag him down.

"When I spoke to Sophie last night, we purposely avoided talking about the memoir, but I can't stop thinking about it. I had to know what they were doing back home, and they're not even panicking. There's no real plan for damage control. They're just going to ride out the storm. Or maybe they've already decided the scandal is easier to live with than a son who doesn't quite fit the mold."

"Well," I say, nudging him lightly with my elbow, "if it's any consolation, I've met you. And the mold's the one that should be nervous."

That gets a smile. Tired, but real. He bumps his shoulder into mine.

"Thanks, Els."

"For what?"

"For sitting on a curb in Colorado in, like, 10 degrees Celsius just to keep me from spiraling too hard."

I wrinkle my nose. "Ew. Celsius? Come on, Ollie, you know I have no idea what temperature that is. Is that warm? Do you think this is a warm morning?"

He laughs— a real one this time—and throws an arm around my shoulders, tugging me closer in a one-armed hug. It's warm, solid, and familiar.

"Thanks for doing this trip with me," he says, his voice quieter now. "Honestly, I think I've discovered another layer of myself I didn't know existed."

I turn toward him, propping my head up with my hand, giving him space to say more. He looks up at the sky again, eyes tracking a plane crossing overhead, its blinking red and white lights moving steadily through the clouds. For a long time, we both watch it until it fades from view.

"I haven't been Prince Oliver here," he says finally. "I've been around people who don't know who I am, don't know my title, and who've still opened their worlds to me. I got to be just an American at a football game. I got to race a lawnmower— which, by the way, I still can't believe is a real thing."

I laugh. "I'm so happy it is!"

"Same. But, I helped drive a tractor, ran through a corn maze, went to a Fall festival… all like a normal person. Not a prince posing for photos. And best of all, I got to do it with you. You really are the best, best friend."

"Okay, stop." I wipe my eyes and tilt my face back to the sky. "You're going to make me cry."

"Make you?" Ollie leans in, eyebrows raised. "Babe, you're already crying."

"You're such a jerk," I mutter, sniffing as I lightly shove his shoulder.

He just smiles—soft, warm, unbothered.

"You're the best, best friend, too, you know." I add.

For a second, we just sit there in silence. Not the awkward kind, but the kind that's full. Full of what we've seen, what we haven't said. The kind of quiet that says, 'I know. Me too.'

After a moment, I speak again, softer this time. "Do you want to talk about it? The memoir stuff?"

He shrugs. The tension creeps back into his shoulders like a weight settling. "It's just… embarrassing. Half of it's exaggerated, and the other half is stuff I wish I could erase. But it's out there now. And once it is, it's not really mine anymore. It belongs to tabloids, press offices, strangers who think they know me."

I nudge him gently, not pushing, just reminding. "But I do. Know you, I mean."

He glances over. His eyes meet mine, and for a beat, the guarded look falters. There's something grateful in his gaze, tinged with sadness, but also relief.

"I know," he says quietly. "That's what makes this trip the best."

We sit there for a while longer as the sky slowly brightens. It's not the dramatic, cinematic kind of sunrise—just a gradual shift from deep navy to gray-blue, then to the muted gold of morning.

The motel door finally creaks open behind us. Noah appears in the doorway, rubbing sleep from his eyes. His hair is a mess, his jacket is half-zipped, and he looks so endearingly disheveled it makes my chest ache.

"I thought I dreamed you two whispering out here like teenagers at summer camp," he mumbles, voice thick with sleep.

"You didn't dream it," I call back. "We were having a deeply emotional moment. You missed it."

Noah raises an eyebrow. "Do I get a recap?"

Ollie groans, pushing to his feet with a stretch. "Only if there's food involved."

I rise too, brushing off my pajama pants, then glance up at him. "You okay?"

Ollie lets out a long breath before nodding. "Yeah. I think I actually am."

We walk back inside, shoulder to shoulder, and for the first time, it doesn't feel like we're just escaping. Not from duty or pressure or lives that never quite fit.

We're moving toward something now. Something real.

CHAPTER 30

U tah's actually pretty interesting," I say, eyes tracing the jagged silhouette of the distant peaks. "The north has these big, beautiful mountains, and the south is all desert. Honestly, you can get almost everything here, except the ocean. But DC doesn't have that either, and I'd trade the Capitol for a mountain hike any day when I'm feeling overwhelmed."

I glance over at Ollie. He's watching me with a look I can't quite decode—eyebrows raised, somewhere between amused and perplexed.

"What?" I ask.

"Are you really talking up Utah now?" he says, shifting his weight against the car. "You realize that every state we've passed through—and no offense, it hasn't exactly been the scenic route—you talk about like it's your favorite?"

I shrug and lean back beside him, the sun-warmed metal of the hood heating my spine. "It's all part of the job, I guess."

A beat passes.

"Besides," I add with a sideways glance, "you're telling me you couldn't do the same for every corner of the Commonwealth?"

"Maybe not in private," Ollie says with a teasing grin, "but definitely in public. Besides, I think I have more room to brag about somewhere like, say, Scotland, than you do for Nebraska."

I bump his shoulder, and he bumps me back, like we've been doing all trip. These small touches don't need explanation—they're wordless agreements, little signals that say, we're still in this together.

The gas station door jingles behind us. Noah steps out, arms full of glossy pamphlets like an overly ambitious camp counselor.

"So," he says, dropping them onto the hood, "the clerk mentioned that at Zion National Park, you have to take a shuttle to get to the main areas. Also," —he flips one toward us— "we're apparently not far from the North Rim of the Grand Canyon. That could be cool to see."

He hands each of us a different brochure.

"What are you guys thinking?" he asks, squinting against the sunlight. "Want to stop and check either out, or just head on to Irvine? Looks like it's just under six hours from here."

Six hours.

Six hours left. Just six hours until this cross-country blur of bad motels, spontaneous detours, diner breakfasts, and car karaoke becomes a memory. Until the most unexpected, chaotic, and strangely freeing experience of my life is over.

I hate that thought.

I glance at Ollie. He's already looking at me, grinning like we're co-conspirators in some delicious secret.

"We're so close," I say, letting the words settle deep in my chest. "It almost doesn't feel real."

"We could be reasonable," Noah says without much emotion. "Push through. Get there by nightfall."

"Or," Ollie counters, flipping his pamphlet over with a spark in his eyes, "we could be completely unreasonable and go float the river."

"Float the river?" I repeat, taking the flyer from him. The front shows people sprawled across oversized, neon-colored inner tubes, drifting lazily down a sun-drenched stream. Their faces are all sun-kissed grins and blissed-out vibes. My skin prickles at the thought of joining them.

"I'm just saying," Ollie shrugs, all casual charm. "It's the most aggressively American summer thing we haven't done yet."

Noah's already shaking his head. "That sounds like a terrible idea. What if your tube flips and you get stuck underneath and drown, and then—boom—I'm beheaded for letting you die on my watch?"

Ollie arches an eyebrow. "Mate, you're really committing to the whole beheading fantasy, huh?"

"I don't know how many ways I can say this," Noah replies, dry as ever, "but I'm fairly certain there would be dire consequences for this commoner if I let anything happen to either of you."

"It's literally a lazy river," Ollie says, deadpan. "People take their toddlers on it."

Noah folds his arms. "Toddlers also eat glue and shove crayons up their noses."

"Okay," I cut in, holding the pamphlet between them like a peace offering. "Let's all take a breath and remember we're talking about floating. On water. In tubes."

"I'm just saying," Noah mutters, "there are safer ways to relax. Plus, it's not even summer anymore. It's probably off-season."

"Alright," I say, passing the pamphlet back to Ollie. "I vote we at least check if it's still open. Personally? I say we do it all—Zion from the car, Grand Canyon if there's time, and one completely safe, utterly chill, float-down-the-river experience."

Ollie points at me like I've just delivered world peace. "This is why she's the brains of the operation."

Noah rubs the back of his neck, clearly torn. His gaze bounces from me to the car, to Ollie, and back again.

"You two realize if either of you ends up on someone's tourist vlog while we're floating downriver in neon tubes, I will spontaneously combust?"

"Well, then we'll just get extra tubes to float your ashes," Ollie says smoothly.

Noah sighs like we've aged him ten years, though a faint smile betrays him. He shoots me a look—you too? I shrug with a grin. I'm in.

"Fine," he mutters. "But if either of you gets sunburned, I'm filing a report."

"With whom?" Ollie asks, all innocence. "The royal sunscreen department?"

I laugh, snagging one of the extra flyers as I head for the car.

"Alright, gentlemen, let's go meet the Virgin River."

Noah calls after me, "Please never say that sentence out loud again."

Ollie laughs at our banter. "Let's hit Zion first, so we're not wet while we're there."

"Now, who's the brains of the operation?" I tease as we reach the car.

The car doors slam shut, the AC hums to life, and as we drive toward the park, I glance out at the endless stretch of road ahead. My chest feels lighter—like I've shed something I didn't even know I was carrying.

There's something about the desert—how it stretches wide and wild, endless and free—that makes it feel like anything's possible.

CHAPTER 31

I think it's best we don't get on a busy shuttle bus," Noah states, and I can't help but agree as he points to a map of the park. "There's still some of the park we can see by car, so we won't get the full experience, but at least we get some. It'll be safer for you both, and there's less chance of your photos popping up online."

We all agree, and as we pull up to the gates and pay the park ranger to enter, that's when the real magic starts. We drive through a long, dark tunnel and suddenly, on the other side, there it is. It feels like we've entered a whole new world. I wish I had my phone—or at least a camera—to capture this. I roll down my window, like the glass is getting in the way of the view, and let the wind rush in, messy and warm. The air smells of sagebrush, sweat, and something else that makes me feel lighter. I take in the towering red rock formations, their jagged peaks cutting into the blue sky. The colors—burnt orange and deep rust—seem to pulse with life, alive in the shifting light.

"I don't think I've ever seen anything like this," I whisper, my voice barely more than a murmur in the stillness.

Noah drives slowly through a line of cars, everyone soaking in the mesmerizing view. We'd love to hike one of the smaller trails up to a lookout, but risking being noticed isn't an option. Instead, we drive a little further until Noah pulls off at a quiet spot with its own lookout and only a couple of cars.

We climb out and follow a narrow path for a better view. For a moment, we stand silently, almost reverently, staring up at the towering rock formations.

"It's really hot here," Ollie breaks the peaceful silence. He takes off his hat and fans himself with it.

I playfully roll my eyes at Ollie, then turn back to the view. The sheer scale of it all overwhelms me a little. The canyon walls stretch endlessly, as if they might touch the heavens. Tilting my head to the sky, I feel smaller than ever, though not uncomfortably so. Actually, it's quite freeing. All my worries, all the daily pressure, seem so tiny, insignificant in the grand scheme of things. A smile spreads across my face as I keep my gaze skyward, feeling the sun's warmth on my skin, the scent of sagebrush around us.

"You look at peace," Noah says, suddenly beside me.

"You know what? I think I am," I admit, turning to him. "Have I thanked you yet? For all this?" I ask with a teasing smile, knowing I've thanked him more times than I can count. Still, it never feels enough.

"All of this? I hate to break it to you, Ellie, but this wasn't my doing. It's actually," he glances at his map of the park, then back at me, "the Virgin River you should thank for forming this."

"You think you're funny, don't you?"

"Yeah, a bit."

Ollie takes in the view, but the poor English boy can't handle the desert heat. After a moment, he says he's going to admire it from inside the air-conditioned car. I watch Noah hand him the keys before turning back to the colorful rock landscape, letting out a sigh of contentment.

"It's so beautiful."

"Yeah." Noah sighs, and when I turn to him, he's looking straight at me. My stomach flips. It's a perfectly cheesy moment, straight from every teen drama I devour—yet somehow, it feels perfect.

"Extremely beautiful."

"That's quite the line, Noah Hart."

He shakes his head and steps closer. "Not a line, just the truth."

The stillness in the air thickens with tension as my attention shifts to Noah's mouth instead of the view.

"Oi! Will you just kiss already so we can get some water? I swear, I can feel the water inside me evaporating. Ever felt that? I'm only about forty percent water now!" Ollie calls from the car.

"Forty percent water sounds alarming," Noah says quietly, just loud enough for me to hear.

"Mmhmm. Imagine feeling like a jellyfish drying out on the beach. Truly horrific."

"I know you're making fun of me!" Ollie shouts. "And

it's not fair, because I can't hear you! Now, come on — three seconds to kiss, or you forfeit your chance."

"He's bossy," I say, looking from Ollie back to Noah. "That's why he's going to be king."

"I don't want to forfeit my chance then." Noah frames my face with his hands and closes the distance, his mouth meeting mine.

Ollie's countdown and watchful eye, the perfect landscape around us, other tourists chatting as they take in the view—it all fades away. All that matters is Noah.

"Alright, you two, there are kids here." Ollie places a hand on Noah's chest and then mine, gently separating us. "Now, you know what would really make this moment perfect? A water."

"I thought you left," I say without breaking eye contact with Noah.

"I was, until you two looked like you were about to scar some poor kids with your lovey-dovey act. Besides, I'm probably thirty percent water by now. We need to fix that immediately."

"You lose water fast. Maybe you should have that checked out," I tease. We agree to give Ollie what he so desperately needs and agree to go get water.

Ollie stumbles back toward the car like he's crossing a desert in search of an oasis. Noah and I linger a moment longer, still close, still slightly breathless.

"You know, it's kind of weird when you think about it—we just kissed in front of the future King of England, in a national park in Utah."

"I think we've done weirder things this week," Noah says, resting his forehead gently against mine for a second before stepping back.

"You're not wrong." I shake my head with a grin.

Back at the car, Ollie sprawls across the backseat, one arm over his eyes like he's auditioning for a soap opera. The drama of this one.

"You two took forever," he groans. "I was starting to think I'd have to flag down a park ranger to rescue me."

I grab a bottle of water from the floor and toss it into his lap. "There, your highness."

"Thank you, peasant."

Noah chuckles at our exchange as he starts the car and pulls back onto the scenic drive, the canyon walls rising around us like something out of a dream. The road curves and dips, bordered by rust-colored cliffs glowing softly in the afternoon sun.

"You know what's weird?" I say after a while, my gaze fixed on the ridges cutting into the sky. "I keep seeing outfits in the landscape."

Noah glances at me. "What do you mean?"

"Like—those cliffs?" I point. "That color would make the most incredible suede jacket. Or that ridgeline—it's got such a dramatic shape. I can see it as a hemline."

Ollie lifts his sunglasses. "Are you hallucinating from heat stroke?"

"Nah," I say, smiling to myself. "I guess it's just a fashion thing. I do this a lot. I see clothes in everything. Even now, without a sketchbook or fabric, my brain just doesn't shut off."

"That's kind of amazing," Noah says, his voice low.

I shrug, but heat blooms in my chest that has nothing to do with the sun. "It's just a hobby. Well, it was—until now. I think I'd be happy making a career out of it. That is, if my parents don't throw a fit and ship me off to some remote island, stuck making clothes from fig leaves."

"They won't," Noah says, eyes on the road but words meant for me alone. "You don't need a degree to be a designer. You already are one."

I blink, my heart fluttering like it only does around him.

"You guys, this place is turning you both into poetic weirdos," Ollie mutters. "Also, I'm still thirsty."

Noah and I laugh. I lean back, the sun warming my face, cliffs rolling by, and Noah's words echoing in my mind—*You already are one.*

CHAPTER 32

The sun casts a shimmering haze over southern Utah's landscape. After some debate—Noah's nerves, Ollie's persistence, and my unrelenting need for one last carefree experience—we all agreed to go tubing. Just outside Zion, we find a sleepy rental stand that doesn't ask many questions. I overhear a crew member telling someone the season should be over, but they're keeping it open a few more weeks. They say it's because of the unseasonably warm weather, but I can't shake the feeling that the universe is making sure we get one more adventure. They hand us oversized neon-orange tubes, a dry bag for valuables, and an "oh, you'll be fine" smile that does nothing to calm Noah.

We're told exactly where to get out of the river—a small bus will bring us back to the lot, or we can walk back easily. Noah studies the posted map, questioning the employees to confirm there are no rough waters ahead. They barely acknowledge him, so Noah returns to us by the riverbank.

"Just stay together," he mutters for the third time, adjusting the dry bag strap across his chest like it's a lifeline. He's definitely muttered under his breath more than once about how it shouldn't be legal to do this without life jackets. "No going rogue."

"Will you relax? We're floating," Ollie says, stepping into the ankle-deep water, already letting his tube drift away a little. "Not storming the beaches of Normandy."

The water is cold—shockingly so after the desert heat—but it feels good. It nips at my calves as I wade in, tube in hand, and I laugh when Ollie slips, his tube flipping before he scrambles to right it.

"Off to a very regal start," I tease, glancing at Noah, who huffs beside me.

"Listen," Ollie grumbles, "royalty aren't built for river sports. Mostly awkward public appearances and waving."

Noah steadies me as I ease into my tube. The rubber's still hot from the sun, but the moment I lean back, toes skimming the water, I let out a long, contented sigh.

"This," I say, arms out like I'm flying, "is perfection."

Noah squints, watching both me and the lazy current as if the river might suddenly betray us, like class five rapids could appear and sweep us away. He's last to get in, lowering himself carefully onto his tube, like it might explode beneath him.

"I hate this already," he mutters, though his voice lacks conviction. His mouth twitches into a smile as he leans back, one hand lazily trailing through the water.

The current tugs us forward slowly, pulling us away from the small launch point and into the river's wider stretch. Red rock walls rise around us—wild, sun-baked—and the cottonwood trees lining the bank offer just enough shade to keep things comfortable. Birds flit overhead, the only sounds the splash of water, occasional giggles from other tubers, and Ollie loudly announcing, "This might be the best decision I've ever made!"

"You say that every time you try a new snack," I call back.

Noah chuckles beside me. I glance over and find him more relaxed than I have all day. His tube bumps softly against mine, the current's gentle sway pulling us closer, then drifting us apart.

"You know, this is the most low-risk thing we've done on this entire trip, yet you're acting like we're floating in a shark-infested warzone."

"You can never be too careful, especially when it comes to Mother Nature."

"You sound like an airport dad."

"What exactly is an 'airport dad'?"

"You know, those dads who have to be at the airport five hours before their flight even boards, who have to control everyone's passports and tickets. Basically, they always have to be prepared, in charge, and stick to a strict schedule."

"Is that meant to be an insult?"

I raise an eyebrow. "You tucked an emergency whistle into the dry bag."

He pauses. "You'll thank me if we get separated."

I grin, shifting in my tube until I'm floating sideways—a better angle to look at him. His dark hair is damp where he splashed water over his head earlier, and tiny droplets cling to his lashes. The sun has warmed his skin, making him look golden, like he belongs under this wide-open sky.

I don't mean to reach over. My fingers just trail out, brushing his hand where it rests in the water between us. He glances down, then up at me, and his easy smile softens into something quieter, more serious.

"What is it?"

He doesn't answer, but hooks his pinky with mine.

"Careful, Noah, or I might think you're falling for me." The words slip out before I can stop them—part tease, part truth, part shield.

Instead of laughing, Noah blinks. And then—he doesn't look away.

"I thought it was obvious I was," he says, matter-of-fact, so sure of himself.

My throat tightens.

Before I can answer, a shout from ahead breaks the moment.

"Come on, lovebirds!" Ollie calls. "You're missing all the excitement—I just floated past a duck family, and one of them hissed at me! Are ducks supposed to hiss?"

We both laugh, the tension easing perfectly. Noah reaches out, grabs one handle of my tube, tugging me closer so we drift side by side again. I place a hand over his.

"Don't let go," he murmurs, voice low, barely carried over the flowing river.

"I wasn't planning to."

The river winds on, its current stronger in some places, gentler in others. We drift beneath low-hanging branches and wave at fellow floaters. Suddenly, Ollie starts singing a song none of us recognize, completely out of tune, insisting it's a Welsh folk tune—though we're pretty sure he's making it up as he goes.

I lean back, letting the sun soak into my skin. For once, I don't care about my frizzy hair or that I'm crammed into a neon rental tube wearing a touristy tank top. I don't mind that I'm without a phone, makeup, or even clean shoes. What matters is this moment: our laughter, the boy beside me, the freedom of floating without expectations, without eyes, without headlines.

Eventually, the river narrows, and the sign for the pull-out point appears up ahead. Other floaters start paddling toward shore, and a pang of disappointment tightens in my chest. I don't want this to end.

"Look at that, we survived. No sharks, no rapids sweeping us away. You were so brave!" I tease.

"You're right. Though I might have gotten a bit of a sunburn."

"Worth it, though."

He tilts his head toward me. "Yeah. Definitely worth it."

We reach the shoreline. Noah jumps out first, steadying my tube with gentle but firm hands on my waist. When I stand, I'm suddenly very aware of how close we are.

He takes my tube, climbing onto the shore after me.

"Hey," he says, dropping the tubes and brushing a wet strand of hair off my face, "just so you know…"

"Mmhmm?" My eyes get lost in his dark ones.

"I didn't just fall. I jumped."

Then he turns and walks toward the tube drop-off, dry bag in hand, leaving me barefoot in the sand with a smile I can't shake.

CHAPTER 33

Though we're just hours away from the Grand Canyon, we decide against going—it's too late by the time we finally make it back to the car after our river float. We're starving and drained from a full day under the sun. Instead, we head to the nearest city, St. George, to find dinner and somewhere to stay.

Tomorrow, we'll reach our destination.

We've planned some time at Disneyland—something I know makes Noah incredibly nervous because of the crowds. We've talked him into going at night, which helped Noah agree. We tried to explain celebrities visit Disneyland all the time without being noticed. It's like New York City—there are so many people that no one stands out. He tried to remind us we're not some stars on TV, but could have people who strongly disagree with my dad's politics or just royals in general, that it's a bigger safety concern.

However, knowing what a dream it is, he's not going to keep us from fulfilling that. We just have to go under the added disguise of the night.

During the day, we'll spend some time at the Pacific

Ocean and, of course, visit Noah's grandma. As we get closer to California, I notice Noah growing more nervous about seeing her. He occasionally mutters that she might not even live where she used to, or that he's not sure if she's still alive. For his sake, I desperately hope both are true.

The Secret Service will sweep in tomorrow or the day after to pull us back to reality. Even though our trip isn't over yet, a weight presses down on me, knowing the end is truly near. Since the maze, we haven't had any run-ins with security. I just hope we get to finish our planned activities—we're so close.

"You okay?" Noah asks, his voice low and steady as he sits beside me on the pool chair.

My eyes stay fixed on the setting sun—the orange and pink sky glowing against the red rocks. It feels like I've stepped into a painting. I don't answer immediately, just nibble my bottom lip, staring at the fading sun. Noah lets the silence hang between us before I finally turn to him.

"It's just… this trip's ending, and I'm not ready to go back to being 'The First Daughter'. I like being just me."

He leans forward, elbows on his knees. "Ellie…" His voice is soft but firm. "You are you. That's not something anyone can take away. You're not a title."

I don't reply, my gaze lifting to the sky above us, watching as stars begin to appear in the darkening night.

Noah's gaze softens, and he scoots closer to share my pool chair. He brushes a strand of hair from my face, his fingers warm on my skin. "Ellie, listen to me," he says, voice steady. "You're someone worth knowing. Not because of your dad or your title, but because of who you are. You're smart, kind, and real. You make people feel seen—I feel seen when I'm with you. You're not just a symbol. You're you. And that's more than enough."

I swallow hard, the lump in my throat making it hard to speak. He really sees me. For everything I am, beyond the role they want to force me into.

"I'm here. I've got you," he says softly, wrapping an arm around my shoulders and pulling me close.

"Noah? For the record, I'm pretty sure I jumped too," I say, returning to our conversation from earlier at the river. "And I think that's another reason I'm having a hard time realizing this trip is almost over. Not having you around all the time."

Noah's hand curves under my jaw, tilting me closer until his lips find mine. I melt into the kiss, but a sharp throat-clearing breaks the moment. We pull apart to see Ollie shaking his head as he strides into the pool area, the metal fence clinking behind him.

"Are you two serious right now? Can you not kiss for like two minutes?" He drops into the chair opposite me, leaning back. "Yeah, I'm not going anywhere. Someone needs to chaperone you two."

Time slips away as we laugh, trading memories from the trip — moments that feel like lifetimes past.

"Tonight could be our last night," Ollie says suddenly, almost springing up from his chair. "And you know what that means."

"I actually have no idea what that means," I reply, raising an eyebrow. "Besides the obvious—for sure a grounding when we get home."

"True," he concedes, then grins. "But no. It means…" He trails off suddenly before cannonballing into the dimly lit pool. "Cannonball!" he shouts, not caring if anyone hears.

Noah and I laugh as Ollie resurfaces, shaking water from his hair and slicking it back with his fingers.

"Come on, kids. Who's next?"

Noah and I exchange a look but don't move to join him.

"Water's nice and warm. Mmm. Just like a hot tub." Ollie splashes lightly. "Come on, First Daughter," he adds with a teasing smirk. "You know you want to."

You know what? Why not. Without another thought, I kick off my shoes, stand up, and launch into my own cannonball. Ollie cheers as I hit the water.

I resurface with a gasp. "This is not hot tub warm, you liar!" I shout, splashing him.

"Relax, you'll get used to it." He splashes me back, then we both turn to Noah. We don't speak — just stare at him, waiting.

Noah crosses his arms. "Oh sure, like I'm going to jump in after Ellie just said it's cold."

"Ollie's right, I'm already used to it. Now come on!" I watch him hesitate. "Don't make me pretend I'm drowning so you'll jump in to save me." I tease lightly.

"Who says I won't just use my emergency whistle to call for help?" Noah counters.

I drop beneath the surface, holding my breath just to mess with him. When I surface, I deadpan, "Noah. I'm drowning."

He sighs softly, but his smile gives him away — he's anything but annoyed as he takes off his shoes.

"Cannonball! Cannonball! Cannonball!" Ollie chants, slapping the water with his hands.

Noah launches into the pool with a cannonball splash, sending waves over the edge. Underwater, he tugs at my ankle, playful and sudden, pulling me deeper with him. I yelp, kick free, and burst to the surface just as he rises beside me.

"Hi," he says, water dripping from his curls, his grin easy. "I heard someone was drowning?"

"False alarm," I say, smiling as he gently brushes wet strands from my face.

Behind us, Ollie groans. "I forgot how much I hate wet jeans."

Noah and I dissolve into laughter.

We spend the next little while racing each other and seeing who can swim the furthest underwater without coming up for air. None of us is particularly good at it, but that's not the point. Eventually, our wet jeans become unbearable—heavy, clinging to our legs like damp seaweed—and we finally drag ourselves out of the pool.

Shivering in the night air, we grab pool towels from a

small wooden stand by the gate. Water clings to our clothes, dripping onto the concrete as we huddle into the fabric.

"Dibs on the shower first!" I shout, wrapping a white towel tightly around me as I bolt toward the room, racing the boys with numb feet and a grin I can't quite wipe off.

CHAPTER 34

We're at a gas station on the outskirts of Las Vegas, the city shimmering in the distance like some random oasis dropped in the middle of nowhere.

I volunteer to pump the fuel while Noah and Ollie head inside to use the restroom and scout out essential road trip snacks.

Leaning over the hood, I start scrubbing the windshield, clearing it of the bug graveyard we've collected. Just as I'm about to finish, Ollie steps outside.

"Here, I'll do that. You go use the restroom," he says, reaching for the squeegee.

I raise an eyebrow. "Wait, does His Royal Highness know how to clean bugs off a windshield?"

He flashes a cheeky grin and takes the tool from my hand. "It's a trip of new experiences. Now go."

Inside the little shop, the air conditioning hits me like a wave of mercy. I scan for the restroom signs and spot them at the back, above a narrow hallway. Two doors sit side by side with a single faded sign in between: Women.

I hesitate. The setup is ambiguous at best. No arrows, no clarity. I glance around for another sign, but nope, this is it. Taking a chance, I push open the left door—

—and find shelves lined with cleaning supplies, toilet paper, and… Noah?

He spins around, startled, and the shock on his face mirrors mine. One hand drops from his cheek. I immediately turn on my heels.

"Sorry!" I blurt, fumbling for the other door, the one that's hopefully the actual women's restroom.

But then, my brain catches up to what I just saw.

I pause.

Something doesn't add up.

I glance back, hesitate, then open the door again. Noah's standing exactly where I left him, and now he's sliding something into his pocket.

"Noah?" I step inside, eyes scanning the cramped room. This definitely isn't the men's restroom.

"I took a wrong turn," he says with a forced laugh. "This isn't the restroom."

"Was that a phone?" I ask, pointing to the thing he just tucked away.

"What?"

"A phone. Were you just on the phone?"

I take a step closer. He doesn't move. Doesn't even blink. And now he looks more cornered than caught off guard.

If it were just a burner, why the sudden defensiveness? Why take a call in a supply closet?

Before he can react, I reach for his front pocket and pull out the object.

It's a phone, all right.

But not just any phone.

It's an iPhone.

"I thought you left this! We're probably being tracked!" Panic rises in my throat. No wonder security keeps popping up like we're in some spy movie.

Almost on cue, the phone vibrates in my hand. Noah reaches for it, but I twist away, holding it out of his reach.

Why do I half expect some girl's name to flash across the screen?

Except… I almost wish it were.

INCOMING CALL FROM MARKS

Time slows. My heart drops.

I glance up at Noah, my vision already blurring. I want to believe there's an explanation — a good one — for why Marks, the head of my personal security, is calling from Noah's phone.

Noah's eyes lock on mine. He looks like he's searching my thoughts, maybe hoping I'll say something first. I can't. I just hand him the phone.

"Answer it."

He doesn't move.

"Answer it," I say again, firmer this time. A command.

Noah closes his eyes for a moment, then swipes to answer.

"Hart," he says, skipping a greeting.

I whisper, "Put it on speaker."

He shakes his head, but I narrow my eyes at him until he exhales, defeated. With a small sigh, he lowers the phone and taps the speaker button.

"–next fuel stop is at the first exit in Barstow, and then—"

I snatch the phone from Noah. "You've been following us? This whole time?"

There's a pause on the other end. "Miss Hastings."

"Since when? Was it the girls at the station in Indiana? Is that when you found us?"

My chest tightens. I knew it was too good to last. "How did you know which route we were taking?"

"Miss Hastings," Marks says, his voice clipped, "if you're finished with your cross-country gallivant, we need to get you home. The Queen's patience is wearing thin, and the fact that the heir to the throne is—"

"How long, Marks?" I cut him off. "How long have you known?"

He's all business, rigid and calm, the kind of voice that sends most people into silence. But not me. I've spent more hours with him than with some of my so-called friends. Sometimes I pretend he is a friend—even though

I know he's paid to monitor me.

"Since the beginning," he says, without hesitation.

I look up at Noah. He won't meet my eyes. His expression says everything.

"You tracked his phone?" I ask, though there's no need to clarify, I'm clearly talking about Noah.

"You've never not been followed, Miss Hastings."

A sharp buzz floods my ears. I shove the phone into Noah's chest and spin on my heel.

"Ellie!" he calls after me as I storm through the store, the world around me blurring, distant.

It's like I'm floating above my body, disconnected. The fluorescent lights smear into streaks as I push through the doors.

Outside, I sprint toward the car. Ollie is already sprawled in the back seat.

I slide into the driver's seat, jam the key in the ignition. Out of the corner of my eye, I catch Noah sprinting toward us.

I hit the lock button just as he reaches the door. He pounds on the window.

Ollie bolts upright. "What's going on?"

I don't answer. I crack the passenger window—barely. Just enough for air, not enough for trust.

"Did you tell my security where we were?" My voice is steel. "Or did they track your phone without your knowledge?"

Noah freezes, his frantic knocking suspended in the air.

"Ellie, please. Just let me in."

"Which one?"

I already know the answer, but the question spills out anyway.

The pieces start clicking together — the times he wandered off alone, the secretive phone calls, the fact that Marks was stored in his contacts. That's not something you'd do if your phone were actually being tracked.

My chest tightens.

"But how? Why? Are they paying you? Were you really that afraid of getting arrested? I told you I'd protect you!"

My voice cracks, raw and rising.

"Let me in," he says gently. "I'll answer everything."

"Els?" Ollie's voice comes from the backseat, soft and uncertain. He's completely unaware why there's the sudden shift between Noah and me.

I ignore Ollie and keep my eyes on Noah, fury cutting through the hurt.

"Screw you, Noah." My glare could knock him over. "You sold us out."

I throw the car into drive and peel out, leaving Noah behind. He chases after us, but stops at the curb as I merge into the stream of traffic. I don't dare check the rearview mirror—whether he's still standing there watching us vanish or has already turned his back, I don't want to know.

From the back seat, Ollie climbs over the console and drops into the passenger seat with a thud.

"Okay, what was that?" he asks, half-laughing, trying to lift the tension.

"Our trusty guide? Turns out he's been working with my security this whole time. Sounds like we've had shadows from the very beginning."

Ollie slumps into the seat. "What? But he helped us shake them. Was he... aware they were tracking him?"

"Yup." I grip the steering wheel harder, my knuckles stiff and white.

Ollie shakes his head slowly, like he's trying to piece together a puzzle that no longer fits. "So this is it, huh? End of the road."

As if summoned by his words, a police car swings onto the road ahead, lights flashing. I glance at the mirror—another one falls in behind us. Sirens are off, but signals are clear.

They're not here to escort us. They're here to stop us.

I'm angry. So incredibly angry. If they've known our whereabouts all along, why not just let us finish the trip? We're so close to the California state line!

Ollie leans over and places a hand on one of mine. "Thanks for being on the run with me, El. You're the best, best friend."

I glance at him, still not pulling over, driving the speed limit as other cars edge to the side, making space for the police. They're probably thinking this is the calmest, slowest "high-speed chase" they've ever seen.

"How long do you think it'll be before we even see a hint of freedom again?"

"My mum will book me into so many social events I won't remember what a day off feels like." He sighs. "Which sucks, because I'd just like to disappear once that memoir hits the shelves."

I slow down and flick on my blinker, pulling off to the side of the road. Within seconds, shiny black SUVs block us in from all sides.

I put the car in park and turn toward Ollie, reaching over to squeeze his hand.

Marks wastes no time. He's at my door, opening it for me before I can react.

I don't want to see him right now. Anger twists inside me—how did he manage to rope Noah into keeping tabs on us?

Did he threaten Noah with jail or some other legal hammer if he refused?

I don't want to consider the other possibility—that Noah reached out to them first.

But deep down, I want to believe he had no other choice.

CHAPTER 35

Your Highness," an agent says as he opens Ollie's door. I don't catch the rest because Marks leans into my open door.

"You okay?" he asks, scanning me like he's searching for injuries.

Physically? Yes, I'm fine.

Emotionally? No, I'm not.

I feel betrayed by someone I really, really liked. I'm disappointed we didn't make it to our final destination, that we won't get to experience Disneyland, or that Ollie won't see the Pacific Ocean.

I nod at Marks as I unbuckle my seatbelt. He guides me toward one of the waiting black SUVs. I spot Ollie being led to another SUV, and we share a sad smile as our doors are held open. I'm sure they're separating us to limit any chance of further scheming.

I climb into the back seat as if on autopilot. No longer carefree Ellie, but Eleanor now. Marks waits until I'm settled before shutting the door behind me. I half expect the lock to click as he walks around the SUV to the passenger seat.

I stare at the back of the driver's seat, nearly in a trance, when hands reach around me to buckle my seatbelt. Surprised, I turn to face the agent, only to see the last person I want right now: Noah.

I fumble to unbuckle, hoping to slip out and away, but Marks is already inside, and Noah's hand reaches over to stop me, as if reading my thoughts.

"Ellie, please." His voice is soft, pleading.

"I don't want him here," I say to Marks and Hutch, who I only just realize is the agent driving.

Hutch glances over his shoulder at me. "Miss Hastings, I know you're not too thrilled with Agent Hart right now, but—"

The buzzing returns, loud and overwhelming, drowning out everything else. Agent? Did he just call Noah an agent?

No.

No.

No! He must be mistaken. Noah can't be an agent. No, because… well, he was working in catering. He looked so surprised to see us. Why would an agent be stuck in catering? It doesn't add up.

But then, it all suddenly clicks. He was undercover while catering. He's been undercover this whole time. Every single thing about him has been a lie.

I look at him, feeling tears sting the edges of my eyes.

"You're security?" My voice breaks, shaky and raw, like my heart is splintering. I feel sick to my stomach.

Marks glances between us, then toward the front, clearly wanting no part of this conversation. Same here.

"Stop the car," I order, making everyone turn their attention to me. "I mean it. Stop the car."

"Miss Hastings, we're on a freeway," Hutch replies calmly. "We can't stop the car."

That excuse doesn't work. We were literally just stopped on the side of the freeway—people stop there all the time for car trouble.

And right now?

Right now, I have a serious problem—Noah is inside my car. Is his name even Noah?

"Stop the car!" I nearly shout, trapped in the confined space.

I need out. Need air — and not the kind shared with Noah. My breathing speeds up like I've just sprinted a race. A panic attack is rising, but all I can focus on is escaping this SUV.

Hutch finally flicks on his blinker, signaling he's pulling over.

"Ellie," Noah starts, but I unbuckle before the car fully stops and reach for the door, only to find it locked.

"I'm riding with Ollie," I say, wiggling the handle, willing it to give.

"Ellie, please just let me—"

"Let me out. Now." My voice cracks between panic and command. Hutch jumps out and comes around to unlock my door.

Thankfully, Ollie's SUV, following behind, pulls over too. I bolt to it and jump into the back seat. Hutch follows, making sure I'm safely inside while he talks to the driver.

"El, what's—" Ollie starts to say, but I lean into his chest and immediately start crying. These aren't dainty little tears either—almost full-body sobs that have Ollie wrapping an arm around me, holding me close and soothingly rubbing my back as I break down.

The car falls silent, everyone listening to my cries. To my heartbreak. Normally, I'd be embarrassed—and I'm sure I'll be mortified later—but right now, there's only this broken, betrayed heart leading the way.

"El, look," Ollie nudges my shoulder after a while. "It's Vegas."

I sit up as we take the exit before the iconic Las Vegas Strip. Tall hotels with their over-the-top themes loom in the distance, while the freeway is plastered with billboards for lawyers and special events.

I spot a sign for Nellis Air Force Base Airport and lean back into my seat. After a few minutes of us silently watching the airport approach through the windows, Ollie reaches over and squeezes my hand.

"Are you okay? Want to talk about it?"

"Not right now." I wipe under my eye, hoping to erase some smeared mascara that's surely run down my face. Maybe it's a blessing that I only packed cheap mascara from a gas station on this trip.

I glance at Ollie's shirt, which has a few mascara stains and water marks. I whisper an apology.

"Don't worry about it." He nudges my shoulder playfully. "On the bright side, we saw some neat sights, and I definitely won the license plate game."

I can't help but laugh. "I'm pretty sure you were the only one playing."

"Sir, you're to call Her Majesty the Queen when we've taken off," an agent sitting in the passenger seat says.

Ollie groans and leans his head back. "Well, at least Sophie will make a lovely queen. As for me? I'm definitely headed for the Tower of London, never to see the sun again. Or worse—she might bring back beheadings."

I smirk. "Hopefully the Tower's dungeon, then. Maybe in fifty years, when I'm allowed outside, I'll come visit."

He grins. "You, me, and Anne Boleyn's ghost. Party of three."

I laugh, surprised by his comment. Ollie has this knack for making me laugh when it feels like the last thing I want to do.

CHAPTER 36

The drive back to the White House from the airport is a blur. I sit silently in the back of the SUV, hands pressed flat against my lap, as if grounding myself, trying not to fall apart. Ollie sits beside me, a steady, unwavering presence—maybe the only steady thing in my life.

I don't look out the windows as the White House looms closer, a fortress of the life I fought so hard to escape. For a few fleeting days, I did.

Passing through the heavily secured gates, my heart sinks deeper with every turn. It's over. And it ended worse than I ever imagined.

My thoughts drift back to Noah—how he'd been there, protecting me, watching over me. But he betrayed me. He was never who I thought he was.

When the car finally stops in front of the entrance, I open the door, my movements stiff, robotic. Marks is quickly at my side, his presence pressing down on me, making the reality impossible to ignore.

I feel like I'm walking towards the gallows, my parents standing there, waiting. The sight that should comfort me instead stings with disappointment.

"Eleanor," Dad says, his voice calm and authoritative as always. "It's good to have you back."

My jaw tightens. I don't want to be here. I don't want to face them—not after everything that's happened, not after they made me believe I was truly running from our security.

"I didn't want to come back," I say flatly, bitterness sharp in my tone. "But you made sure I didn't have a choice."

Mom steps forward, her face tight with concern, but I keep my gaze fixed on my feet, refusing to meet hers. Not now. She'd see straight through my bitterness to the broken heart beneath it, if she hadn't already.

"You can't keep running from this, Ellie," she says softly.

The weight of the last few days crashes over me in waves, and my eyes sting with tears. "I thought... I thought maybe for once I could choose what to do with my life."

Dad's expression softens, though tension still lingers around his eyes. "This isn't a choice you get to make, Princess. Not when it comes to your safety. We never wanted this for you, but sometimes your role is bigger than you."

I clench my fists at my sides, the sting of Noah's betrayal still raw, cutting deeper than anything else. An overwhelming emptiness floods me as the walls of the White House close in, the weight of my situation pressing heavy on my shoulders.

"Then maybe I don't want any part of it," I spit out, my voice cracking. "Maybe I'm tired of being the 'first daughter,' the symbol. Maybe I'm just tired of being everything everyone else wants me to be."

I turn away sharply and spot Ollie down the hall, speaking quietly with his security team. A desperate wish wells up inside me — that we could just walk away from all this and start over. Begin a new adventure that doesn't involve—

"Ellie." The voice calls from behind me. I freeze, my heart stuttering in my chest. I know that voice. I hate how much I want to find comfort in it.

My pulse races, the ache of his presence nearly unbearable. I thought maybe he'd stayed behind in Vegas after I managed to avoid him on the plane, but there's no denying that voice.

I turn slowly, my face stiff, eyes undoubtedly rimmed red from the storm inside me.

Noah stands at the entrance, his expression a mix of regret and guilt. He's wearing his usual jeans and t-shirt, his face still faintly sun-kissed from yesterday's outdoor activities. He looks like my Noah—and that makes it hurt even more.

He opens his mouth to speak, but I hold up a shaky hand to stop him.

"Don't," my voice cracks, anything but steady as I take a step back. "Don't say anything. You've said enough."

Noah tries to protest, but I shake my head. I don't want to hear any more excuses. The person I trusted, the one I thought was different, the one I really liked—who I hadn't just fallen for, but jumped for—had lied to me. Had betrayed me. And I can't forgive him. Not yet.

"Ellie, I never wanted to hurt you. You have to know that."

"Hurt me?" I repeat, my voice rising. "You lied to me, Noah. For days, I thought I was actually escaping my life, that I was just... me. And you've been watching me the whole time. I was assigned to you!"

Tears finally spill over, streaming down my cheeks as I angrily swipe them away.

Noah steps forward, eyes pleading. "You don't understand. I wanted to let you have that. I did. But my job—my first responsibility-is to protect you. You're the first daughter. You're not just some girl with dreams of running away. You have a duty to this country, Ellie."

My chest tightens. Everything I thought I knew about the past few days shatters into pieces.

"So, all of it was a lie?" I demand, my voice cracking—something I hate but can't stop. "All the time we spent together? All those moments when I actually felt like I could be normal... like I could just be with you—was that just part of your job too?"

Noah's face tightens with pain, his lips pressing together as if searching for the right words.

"I never meant for it to be that way, Ellie," he finally says, his voice quieter now, but still heavy with regret.

"I've never seen you as a job. But I was hired to keep you safe. That's who I am. I'm not just Noah, the guy who drove you off in a catering van. I'm a Secret Service agent. I've been trained for this."

His words hit me like a hammer to the chest. I straighten up, switching into media-ready Ellie.

"Well, Agent Hart," I say, steadier than I feel, catching the flash of hurt in Noah's eyes at the formality. "Thank you for your service."

Before he can reply, I turn and walk away, hating that as I flee down the endless White House corridors—my home, the place that's supposed to be mine—I feel like nothing more than a pawn in a game I never chose to play.

CHAPTER 37

Ellie," Noah says as I pass him in the hallway.

"Oh, Agent Hart. Hello." I plaster on a mega-watt smile, the furthest thing from real. Noah recoils as if I've slapped him.

It's been just over a week since we returned to the White House, since the road trip was cut short, since I discovered the truth about Noah. And worse? I don't even have Ollie here to lean on. He's caught up in his own drama with the impending release of the memoir.

"Can we talk, please?" Noah's voice is pleading. It takes everything in me to fight my instincts and agree. I want to be close to him, to talk, but it feels like he's taken a steak knife, stabbed it into my heart, pulled it out, and plunged it back in every time I'm near him.

"I don't think we have anything to talk about." I try to sound completely unbothered, though inside I'm fighting every urge to move closer to him. This is why I've been avoiding him for the past week, but it hasn't been as easy as I hoped.

"I never meant to deceive you, Ellie. I just wanted to protect you. I wanted to give you the space you needed."

He steps closer, his voice soft, as if hoping for a calm and reasonable conversation. "But when I started getting to know you, when we started talking—"

"Don't." My voice is sharp, cutting him off. I step back, trying to create distance from the suffocating feeling building inside me. "I don't want to hear any more excuses. This—this was never about me, was it? It was always about duty. Your duty. I was just another mission."

Noah's face falls, his eyes pleading for me to understand. "Ellie, you're not just a mission to me. You're not. But I made a promise to your parents, to this country. I had to keep you safe. I *want* to keep you safe."

"Right, well, again, thanks for keeping me safe." I strip away any emotion, knowing we'll never truly see eye to eye—not now, not while the hurt is still so fresh.

"Look, Agent Hart, I'm sorry to cut this conversation short, but I," I glance around the hallway, my eyes flicking over a few stationed guards before returning to Noah, "have a date." The words tumble out before I even comprehend them.

"A date?" Noah's jaw tightens, his hands clenched at his sides.

Well, guess I have to go with this lie now. I guess we're two people who just lie to each other.

"Um, yeah, a blind date. Something my mom's friend set up."

I'm toast. I know it because I never go anywhere alone! How am I supposed to have a date without him finding out it was a complete sham?

"So, uh, yeah, I better be going. Have a nice night, Agent Hart." I spin on my heels quickly, changing course from my original destination—the library—to my mom's office.

Mom's friends are always trying to set me up, whether it's actual dates or just dancing at different events. Surely one of them has someone I can go out with tonight, if I can even convince Mom to let me leave the White House.

I turn down the hallway and disappear from Noah's sight. I lean against the wall and take a deep breath, slowly letting it out. No, this is crazy. I can't go on a date! I'm still recovering from having my heart run through a blender. The last thing I want right now is to fake enjoyment on a date. Maybe I'll fake being sick, that could work! A migraine or, better yet, period cramps. Yes, bingo! No one will question cramps.

I walk toward Mom's office, nodding at her secretary outside before knocking and stepping in. A large vase filled with bright, assorted flowers sits on a coffee table, and red, white, and blue throw pillows give the room a warmer, more welcoming feel than the Oval Office.

"Hey, Mom, you know how your friends seem way more invested in my dating life than I am?" I say, instead of a greeting.

Mom looks up from the sofa where she's reviewing some documents. She pushes her reading glasses onto the top of her light brown hair, giving me her full attention.

"Yes?" She sets the papers aside.

I settled on the arm of a nearby chair to face her. I know

this is far from what she expected me to bring up.

"Do you think any of them could set me up with someone tonight? Just something simple — like ice cream or something."

"A date? Tonight? You do remember you're grounded, right?"

"Oh, darn, you're right. Okay, well, if anyone asks or says anything, can you just tell them I did have a date tonight but didn't feel well?"

I stand up, but Mom gives me a look that makes me sit back down.

"Ugh, fine," I crack under her gaze. How do moms have so much power without saying a word?

"I may have lied to Noah—er, Agent Hart—about having a date tonight. You know, the White House is nothing if not a small town of gossip."

I don't know why it matters, honestly. Noah lied to me on a much larger scale.

It matters because you want him to think you're not pining for him the way you so hopelessly are.

"Ellie," Mom starts, but I hold up a hand to stop her.

"I know, I know. I don't know why I said it, okay? It just—boom—came out before I even realized it."

"Making an agent jealous isn't going to work the way you think it will."

"I know." I plop fully onto the chair. "I don't even think it was jealousy I was feeling. I think… I just don't want him to realize how much he's broken my heart. That I can move on, but he can't."

Mom gives me a look like she understands, and I mentally tuck it away to ask her sometime about her own heartbreaks. To ask how she ever got past them, if she ever did.

"Mom, I was thinking…" I pause, trying to find the best way to say this. Then I decided to just go for it. "I want to do something for a few people we met on our trip. Would that be okay?"

"Such as?" She leans back into the couch.

I nibble on my bottom lip. "Well, I can't stop thinking about this waitress, Sidney. She's working at a run-down diner to pay for college and said she still has a long way to go. Do you think we could create a scholarship for her? I hate seeing someone who desperately wants to attend school but can't because of finances."

"I suppose we could look at that, sure. Was that all? You said a few people."

"Oh, the others are less extensive. I, uh, need to return items to Matt the mower — his jacket, his helmet, and maybe pay for whatever damage we caused to his mower when we jumped off and let it keep going. Or, maybe just get him a whole new mower."

Mom sighs softly at the reminder of Ollie and me fleeing security on a lawn mower. I smile at her.

"I'd also like to do something for a guy named Hank. His auto shop was where we got our car fixed, and he was so kind. He showed me how to check and fix things on a car, and he knew we didn't have much money, so he gave us a heavy discount. I'm not sure what I could do for him — maybe give him some new equipment or a check so he can do any upgrades himself?"

"You know it's not that easy, right? Funding these little gifts for your new friends."

"I know, I know. But with your okay, I'd like to try to make it happen at least."

Mom smiles. "Of course, you have my okay."

CHAPTER 38

Thankfully, it doesn't take long to make it a reality.

We start with Sidney and work our way back.

As we step into the diner, I feel like a reality TV star with my security flanking me like a camera crew. I want to sit and eat, but the rules are clear—these visits are approved as a one-day-only thing. Pretty sure they think there's less chance of me running off that way.

I scan the restaurant, searching for a familiar face. She told me she works a lot, so I assumed she'd be here. Everyone's eyes are on the girl walking in with a crew of well-dressed men, and I've never felt more out of place.

The place is full of truckers in flannel and elderly couples who aren't even trying to hide their stares behind their coffee mugs. Metal utensils scrape across plates, and a low hum of an '80s song plays overhead.

"Do you see her?" Marks asks quietly beside me.

I shake my head, just about to ask another waitress if Sidney's on shift, when she steps out from the back, juggling plates of breakfast food. Her feet falter when she sees us, and for a moment, I panic that she doesn't recognize me. The one time I'd like someone to recognize me, and I worry she doesn't!

Thankfully, that worry is fleeting.

"Hey, you," she says, purposely avoiding my name. "Take a seat, and I'll be right with you."

I head to the back corner booth, trying to avoid as many stares as I can. Marks follows me, while one guard stays near the door and the others remain outside. Definitely overkill—but I'm not in a position to put up a fight about it.

Sidney finally sets her plates down at their designated tables and walks over. I'm sitting on the edge of the booth, and Marks remains posted beside me.

"Hi. I can't believe you're back!" Sidney grins, glancing at Marks. "With a different crew this time."

Ugh. I try not to think about the last time I was here—the awkward, rejected kiss, the ridiculous waffle hut Ollie tried to build. I intentionally sit on the opposite side of the diner from our last table to avoid walking down that specific memory lane.

"Yeah, hey. I'm not staying, I just wanted to give you something." I pat the other side of the table in a silent invitation for her to sit.

She hesitates, eyeing the diner.

"Please. It'll only take a minute."

Thankfully, she sits, curious and confused.

"I know the last time I was here, we didn't talk for long," I say, "but you mentioned wanting to go to school. That you've been working nonstop to make it happen."

Sidney nods. "I remember. Right after you swooped in and saved me when my button tried to leap to its death."

I smile at that and pull an envelope from my bag, sliding it across the table.

"I want you to have this."

She stares at the envelope, her name scrawled across the front, then picks it up like it might cut her.

Thanks to the Secret Service, I'd managed to get her full name—along with Matt's and Hank's—which made everything so much easier.

I watch her brows furrow, then shoot upward as her eyes go wide.

"Are you serious?" she whispers, like saying it any louder might make it vanish.

"I am," I grin, and her eyes fill instantly with tears. I stand and move around the table to hug her.

"Congratulations, Sidney. You're the first-ever recipient of the Eleanor Hastings Scholarship. It covers all four years—tuition, books, food, and housing."

She clutches me tightly, tears finally falling.

"Why?" she asks.

"Because you inspired me. You deserve to chase your dreams, Sidney. You should have the chance to earn that degree and go after the life you want."

She pulls back, wiping her cheeks with her palm. "I don't know how I can ever thank you. Truly. Thank you so, so much."

"You can thank me by inviting me to your graduation in four years." I give her hand a squeeze.

"Deal," she laughs through her tears. "Can I at least get you something to eat?"

"That's okay, we've got to get going," I say, giving her one last hug. "Enjoy school, Sidney."

Next stop is Matt's.

Matt isn't getting a scholarship or a year supply of bacon, but I still want to thank him for letting us escape on his mower.

It's kind of surreal, standing here with some of the same people who were chasing me that day.

We pull up to his house, and I spot the Lightning McQueen mower parked inside an open barn. Marks and another guard each grab a box—one with the gear we borrowed, the other with the gift I brought.

I ring the bell. An older woman answers, and a moment later, Matt appears beside her in the doorway.

"Hi, Matt. Remember me?" I grin. "The girl who hopefully didn't destroy your mower."

He steps forward, eyeing us with suspicion.

"Yeah, I remember. Crazy ex-boyfriend, right?" he says, clearly unconvinced by the original story.

"Right," I laugh. "We brought your stuff back." I nod

toward the box. "And I got you something as a token of appreciation—a set of tools. Heard it's a good brand. Hope it helps, especially if we caused any damage."

Two agents hand over the tools and his belongings.

"Wow, thanks. I didn't think I'd ever see any of this again."

"I hope you win that year's supply of bacon next time," I joke, referencing part of the prize.

"Matty, that's Eleanor Hastings," says the woman behind him.

Matt turns to her, then back to me, recognition lighting up his face.

"The President's daughter?"

"Guilty," I say, offering a sheepish smile.

"I voted for your father, dear. And I'll vote for him again," she says proudly.

"Well, thank you—both for the vote and for letting us borrow Matt for a bit." I shake her hand, sliding into full First Daughter mode with practiced ease.

"This is my grandma," Matt says, slinging an arm around her. "She's a big fan."

After a few more moments and a quick selfie with Matt and his grandma, we're off to our final stop.

Hank's a state away, but thanks to our private plane and a short drive, we arrive in no time. As we pull up to Hank's Auto Shop, I'm already halfway out of the car before it even stops.

"Hank!" I call out, spotting him in his garage, wiping his oily hands on a grubby towel. "Remember me? The girl who shadowed you when our car broke down a few weeks ago?"

"Of course I remember you, darlin'. No more car trouble, I hope?" he says, coming over and pulling me into a hug like a long-lost grandpa.

"Nope. I actually came to see you." I take an envelope from Marks, similar to the one I gave Sidney, and hold it out to Hank. "This is for you."

He raises a bushy brow, wipes his hands on the rag again, then accepts the envelope with his calloused fingers. As he reads, his expression shifts—curiosity fading into surprise, then something softer.

"This is…" He glances up, eyes just a little glassy. "This is a grant."

Thankfully, with a bit of lobbying—okay, arm-twisting—a certain chief of staff managed to revive the so-called White House Discretionary Community Fund. That's how I got Hank this grant.

"It is," I say, smiling. "To support your work, or fix up the garage, or get better equipment—or honestly, whatever you need. You opened your space to us without hesitation. You gave us your time and kindness without knowing who we were. I just wanted to say thank you in a way that mattered."

He exhales slowly, and for a moment, the only sounds are birds chirping and a car rumbling down the road behind us.

"Well, darlin', I don't even know what to say." His voice is thick, like he's trying to swallow his emotions. "This kind of thing doesn't happen to people like me."

"It should," I say simply. "You help people. You deserve this."

"Thank you," he says as we pull apart. "I'll make sure this gets used right. You've got a good heart, Eleanor Hastings."

"So you do know who I am?" I give him a surprised smile.

"I must admit, I didn't at first. But I saw your pop on TV the other day, and that's when I realized."

"Well, make sure you name a wrench after me or something," I tease. "Or at least the car lift."

He chuckles. "Deal. And if you ever find yourself stranded again, you know where to come."

I step forward and give him a hug. He squeezes me tight, like he means it.

Marks holds the SUV door open for me, and I give Hank one final wave as we slowly pull away.

Even though it was just three quick stops, something in my chest feels fuller — like I got to make something right, or at least give a little back to the people who showed me kindness when they didn't have to.

All I'm missing, however, is the one who truly showed me kindness on this trip. The one who changed me. The one I can't stop wanting to seek out, even through the ache.

Maybe one day, it won't hurt so much to see him in the halls.

The next morning, however, is not that day.

"Ellie."

I'm in the library, scanning the shelves for something to read. Most of the books are America-centric in one way or another — history, literature, even philosophy. Still, a few scattered classics are tucked between all the patriotism.

My heart stops. Then starts again at double speed. I turn slowly toward the sound of his voice.

"Agent Hart," I say, forcing a smile. Lately, fake smiles are all I can manage.

Except yesterday—with Sidney, Matt, and Hank. Those smiles were real.

"Good morning."

Noah takes a step closer. "I wanted to thank you. For not getting me fired."

Right. That's his takeaway.

Sidney gets a scholarship.

Matt gets new tools.

Hank receives a grant.

And Noah… Noah gets to keep his job.

Doesn't feel like a gift, more like a consolation prize.

"Why? You were just doing your job, right?"

"Ellie," his voice tightens with something like regret.

But I grab the nearest book off the shelf and step around him before he can say anything else.

I have this sinking feeling that this is how it's always going to be now, him trying to explain, and me doing everything I can not to listen. No more easy conversations. No more heartfelt confessions under the night sky or half-laughing arguments in the car. Just plain formality.

"Have a good day, Agent Hart," I say over my shoulder, trying to flee the library as quickly and politely as possible.

I'm trying to be civil, to tolerate being around him. But it hurts.

That's it. I'm never allowing myself to fall for anyone again if this is how it's going to feel.

I don't slow down until I'm around the corner. Only then do I allow myself to breathe. I glance down at the book in my hand.

Romeo and Juliet.

Of course.

A humorless laugh escapes me. I think back to the game we played on the road trip—would you rather be in love and never be together, or never fall in love at all?

Noah and I picked the same answer: to be in love but never be together.

The Montagues and Capulets.

A First Daughter and her bodyguard.

It's poetic.

It's tragic.

It's fitting.

I retreat to my room, book in hand, and locate the emerald velvet dress I'd kept from the thrift store.

I try not to think about that day—the perfect one. The first time I kissed Noah. Ollie in that ridiculous mint green suit.

A smile tugs at my lips as the memories wash over me, even as a few tears slide down my cheeks.

I let myself feel it—just for a moment: the ache of missing that time, wishing I could step back into it, even if only for a second. I run my fingers over the fabric, determined to give the dress the glow-up it deserves.

I remove the buttons and open my sewing kit, but then I just stare at it, frozen.

Taking a deep breath, I slide off the bed.

It's time to talk to my parents.

CHAPTER 39

The sound of my heels clicking against the marble floors of the West Wing is nearly drowned out by the pounding of my own heart. I practiced this speech in the mirror a hundred times. I ran through every possible scenario with Ollie, and he's excellent at imagining the worst-case ones.

But now, standing outside the Oval Office, my stomach is doing Olympic-level gymnastics that would give Simone Biles a run for her money.

I hesitate, lightly tracing one of the lines on my palm—the same one the fortune teller had pointed out. She also told me I was the magician, that I had the power all along.

I exhale, square my shoulders, and nod a greeting at an agent before pushing open the door and stepping inside.

Dad sits at his desk, his red tie loose, rubbing his temples like he's been on back-to-back calls with world leaders all day. Mom's on the couch, reading briefing notes with the same intensity she'd show when choosing the next Ambassador to the UN.

They both look up as I come in.

"Eleanor," Dad says, straightening. "Everything okay?"

"Yes," I say quickly, then realize my voice sounds a little too forced. "I mean… yes."

Mom sets her notes aside. "What is it? What's going on, honey?"

I take a deep breath. Just say it. Rip off the Band-Aid.

"I've decided on my major."

Dad relaxes, smiling as he leans back in his chair. "That's wonderful! What did you decide? Political Science? International Relations? Maybe Law? You do love debating." He chuckles to himself.

I clear my throat. "Actually, I've decided on fashion design."

Silence.

A very long silence.

A silence so long, I think Dad's term as President is nearly over.

Mom blinks. Dad stares at me like I've just announced I'm running away with the circus.

"Fashion design," he repeats slowly, as if he misheard me.

"Yes." I square my shoulders, forcing myself to sound confident. "I want to study fashion. It's something I love, and I think I could actually make a career out of it."

Mom finally speaks. "Ellie, sweetheart… fashion is a wonderful interest. But is it something you really see yourself doing long-term?"

"Yes."

Dad leans forward, lacing his fingers together on top of his desk. "This is a big decision, kid. You grew up in politics. You understand the world stage better than most adults in my Cabinet. You could do anything—why choose something so… so—"

"Unimportant?" I finish, my voice sharper than I intend.

His brows furrow. "That's not what I said."

I cross my arms. "But that's what you meant. It's what you think."

Dad sighs, rubbing his chin. "Eleanor, your name carries weight. People will expect you to follow a certain path."

"I know that." My voice rises before I can stop it. "That's all my life has ever been—what people expect. But this? This is mine. I want to do something I actually love, not something just because I'm some political nepo-baby."

Mom presses her lips together, her expression unreadable. Dad glances at her, then back at me.

After a long moment, he exhales. "You really want this?"

"I do."

His shoulders drop slightly. "Then I guess we'd better start looking at the best fashion schools."

I blink. "Seriously?"

Mom shakes her head, but there's a hint of a smile. "Ellie, we may not understand this choice, but we'll support you. We'll always support you."

For the first time since stepping into this office, I breathe.

Dad smirks. "I expect free suits for life, though."

I grin. "You and Ollie alone will keep me in business."

"Ellie, honey, while you're here, there's something else we need to talk to you about," Mom says, her serious tone making my smile falter. She glances at Dad, and I follow her gaze.

"It's about Agent Hart, Princess." Dad's voice matches Mom's gravity.

At the mention of Noah, everything slows down, as if time is bending to stretch out the agonizing moment.

"What…" I clear my throat, trying to seem unbothered. "What about him?"

"Eleanor, you got as far as you did because of Agent Hart. He kept us updated, knowing we needed constant whereabouts, or else we were pulling the plug on your little rebellion extravaganza."

I roll my eyes. "Really, Dad? That's what we're calling it?"

"I'm just saying, maybe don't be so hard on him because he's the reason you even got to go. He fought for the plan, knowing you and Oliver would keep trying your escapes until you got what you wanted. You were with a trained agent and had operatives trailing you at all your stops the entire time. They weren't all in suits and black SUVs, though; several were like Agent Hart, in normal cars and civilian clothes."

I hate how the puzzle pieces fit together, because, of course, we were always under the microscope we fought so hard to escape. How could I have truly thought otherwise while out there?

"He lied to me," I say, hating how my voice starts to shake.

"You wanted your freedom. He helped give it to you."

Mom stands and comes towards me, wrapping me in her arms. "Sweetie, is this really about not knowing he was an agent, or is it something else?"

As her arms close around me, my eyes fill with tears, but I refuse to let them fall. "He made me feel seen and important. Not just because of who I am, but because of who I *am*. I felt like Ellie to him, not First Daughter Eleanor Hastings." I let out a small sigh. "I was falling for him, I really was, but all along I was just an assignment."

Even as I say it though, I know it's a lie. I didn't—nor currently am—falling for Noah. Just like I had told him, I jumped.

"If it's easier, I can reassign him, send him elsewhere."

"No, I don't want him to lose his position just because I couldn't sort out my feelings."

Which would be true even if he hadn't just thanked me

for not getting him fired—or, I guess, not fired, just reassigned—but still.

"Honey," Mom gently wipes a tear off my cheek with the pad of her thumb, so much for refusing to cry. "I've seen how he looks at you when you're nearby. You weren't just an assignment."

"Which, to be fair, is rather conflicting for me," Dad adds. "Do I move him to a different team because of his attachment, or keep him because I know now, more than ever, he'd do anything to keep you safe?" Dad looks at me, trying to gauge my thoughts on the matter.

I give him a small, helpless shrug. "I'm not sure. Just don't relocate him. Protecting the President or their family is the dream for agents. Please don't take that away from him."

"You still really care about him, don't you?" Mom plays with a strand of my hair as she asks softly. I give her a broken smile.

"I'm trying really hard not to."

CHAPTER 40

I sit cross-legged on the bathroom counter, applying makeup for one of Dad's endless campaign fundraisers tonight. My phone is on speaker beside the sink, Ollie's voice filling the room as I lean into the mirror to perfect my winged eyeliner.

"So, everything with the memoir seems to be under control?"

Ollie groans. "Is it bad I'm hoping for some tragic event on release day so that takes over the media instead of this stupid memoir?"

I blink, pulling back from the mirror. "Well, yeah, actually. Wishing for a catastrophe isn't exactly the best coping strategy."

"I know, I know," he sighs. "It's just hard knowing exactly the picture it's going to paint. I keep telling myself that if no one within 'the Firm' is concerned, maybe I shouldn't be either."

Ollie often refers to anyone under the royal family's umbrella as 'the Firm,' like it's a company he never asked to be employed by—which, to be fair, it kind of is.

"It's just someone wanting a check and fifteen minutes of fame, Ol," I assure him, brushing some powder under my eyes. "You know that. And tragic distraction aside, it'll be the story for about a week before something new takes over. You more than anyone know how quickly the news cycle moves."

"Yeah," he exhales. "You're right."

"Thanks. I usually am." I tease, trying to lift his mood.

"Not always. What about Noah? And you know, the whole avoiding him like he's the plague thing you've got going on?

I freeze mid-swipe. "You know why."

"I'm just saying, El, he misses you," Ollie says gently.

I pause, staring at my phone like Ollie's face might magically appear on the screen. "You're… you're talking to him?"

"Yes. Because I'm a mature adult who knows how to communicate."

I roll my eyes, even though he can't see me. "Come on, Ol. You think I don't want to? I just… You know how much I like him—or, I guess, liked?" I tilt my head up to the ceiling with a groan.

"You're not fooling anyone with that past tense."

"Yeah, I know," I say, almost sadly. "I just… I hate that it feels like betrayal. From him! I felt so seen with him, Ollie."

"Babe, he's Secret Service, not some Oscar-winning

actor. That wasn't an act. He did—and does—see you for you. Honestly, I'm kind of grateful to him. He made that trip happen. He helped us escape his own guys, because even though they agreed to let us on this adventure, if they caught us, they were bringing us back. He made sure we got to go further. Safely. He gave us something real, El."

"You're really team Noah, aren't you?"

"I'm team Ellie, and as captain of team Ellie I know how he made you feel. And sure, he didn't tell us what he really does for a living. But if you think about it, that wasn't a betrayal. Because if we had known he was actually an agent, we wouldn't have gone. He wanted that trip, not for us, not really. He wanted it for you."

I stare at my reflection in the finger-smudged mirror, Ollie's words bouncing around in my head like a secret I already knew but didn't want to admit.

"I wish you were here, Oliver Oil."

"Me too, Ellie Belly. Now go knock 'em dead. If you get the chance to talk with Noah, do it. There's no reason for you both to be miserable when you want the same thing."

"When did you get so wise?"

I can practically hear his smug grin. "Excuse me, I've always been wise. You're just finally noticing."

After my phone call with Ollie, I got dressed.

Tonight feels like the perfect opportunity to debut the velvet emerald dress I found at the thrift store—of course, now with my own Eleanor Hastings touch. I kept the long sleeves but added elastic at the cuffs so they flare out softly. I hemmed it to hit just above the knee and took in the waist for more shape. The neckline gave me the biggest debate, but in the end, I went with a high neck, clean and classic.

To put it simply, the dress is simple but elegant. Regal, even.

It's perfect.

With one final look in the mirror, I head out to meet my parents.

The campaign fundraiser, like all the others, is a test of my acting skills. I paste on my brightest smile—the kind that says I'm thrilled to be here, even though I'm not.

I poke half-heartedly at the overpriced chicken on my plate. A single plate at this event costs more than most people's weekly pay, yet it tastes like rubber. I'd much rather hit a drive-thru and buy something I'd actually eat for less than ten dollars.

I think about my panic drive-thru ordering and, for what has to be the thousandth time, my gaze drifts across the ballroom.

There he is.

Noah. Except he's not *my* Noah. Not the boy who snuck me all the pink Starbursts and kissed me beneath stars we weren't supposed to see. Tonight, he's Agent Hart—in a sleek black suit, shiny shoes, standing tall and expressionless against the far wall.

My stomach twists. I snap my attention back to my

plate. My skin burns knowing he's nearby. I picture the crinkles beside his eyes when he smiles, the sound of his laugh, the feel of his mouth on mine—and nope.

No! I shouldn't be thinking like this. I try to shake the thought loose.

But I miss him. I miss him, and he's only a few feet away.

"Honey, are you okay?" Mom leans in, her voice quiet against the hum of clinking silverware and polite chatter.

"Mmhmm," I smile wider as I face her. "This chicken is delicious, right?" I make a show of taking a big bite, regretting it immediately, unable to stop my face scrunching up as I chew. Mom lets out a surprised laugh and quickly covers her mouth with her red cloth napkin.

I continue picking at my dinner until a waiter finally rescues me and takes my plate. Dad steps onto the small stage to deliver his speech before the band begins to play. All I want is to crawl into bed and binge terrible reality TV until I pass out.

Instead, I sit folding my cloth napkin into what might be an origami swan—or a napkin disaster—when someone clears their throat beside me. I jerk my head up, heart racing, half-hoping to meet familiar deep brown eyes. But it's not Noah.

It's the grandson of a donor, smiling nervously as he asks me to dance.

I don't want to. But, as always, I smile and say yes.

He leads me to the dance floor where a handful of

couples sway gently to the music. We're at least a decade younger than anyone else there. I place one hand on his arm, the other in his, and try to focus.

He's cute, objectively—curly brown hair, warm hazel eyes, and a kind smile that makes it easy to smile back. In another world, I'm sure I'd actually enjoy this.

But I can feel Noah's gaze pressing against my back like a weight.

I try to ignore it, keep my head in the moment, and pretend I'm not hyperaware of every step I take and every glance I steal toward the wall. But it's no use. Eventually, I cave and look.

Noah's eyes are locked on me.

His posture is rigid, jaw clenched, like he's holding himself back from doing something reckless. Maybe— just maybe—he wants to cross the room and cut in. Maybe even punch the guy dancing with me.

Okay, that might be wishful thinking, but he definitely doesn't look pleased.

I glance at the other Secret Service agents. All of them look equally stiff, equally blank. It's literally their job to show no emotion.

I let out a small sigh because clearly it *is* just wishful thinking. But then again, it feels like Noah's trying a little too hard.

"Everything okay?" my dance partner asks, clearly noticing my sigh.

Poor guy. I don't even know his name.

I force myself to focus on him through the rest of the dance, though it takes more effort than it should. When the song ends, I thank him politely and lead him toward one of the bubbly girls I met earlier tonight. She's charming, warm, and might actually enjoy his company more than I can right now. It's a small way to apologize for being completely distracted during our dance.

Then, my eyes find Noah again.

It hits me like a wave: I feel like I'm suffocating.

I'm not sure I can do this anymore. I can't keep pretending. Can't keep pretending I don't know him, that I'm not completely consumed by thoughts of him, that he's just another suit standing against a ballroom wall. He's not.

He's everything.

And I'm not sure I can keep pretending he's not.

CHAPTER 41

I need air.

This room feels too small, the walls somehow closing in tighter by the second. I hurry to the door where Noah stands, but don't look at him as I rush out. I lift the hem of my knee-length dress and start to run. My heels echo down the hall, clinking against the tiled floor. I race past guards posed so firmly it's like they're statues. I feel like a runaway bride.

"Eleanor?"

A familiar voice calls behind me. I slowed to a stop, taking a deep breath before turning to face Marks.

"I'm not running, I mean I am literally running, but I'm not, like, escaping. Okay? I just need…" I trail off, my voice caught in my throat as my eyes start to water.

Marks takes a step closer, concern etched on his usually stoic face. I raise my hands, palms out, to stop him.

"I'm okay. Really." It's a lie, and the way Marks studies me, he knows it.

"I need…" I try to finish again. What do I need?

I need air.

I need quiet.

I need Ollie here.

I need to be alone, even though I don't think alone is truly what I want. Not unless I'm alone with Noah.

Ugh. What I really need is a time machine to take me back to never having met Noah. To before I fell… no, nope. We are not going there, Eleanor Elizabeth!

I look up at Marks, almost in fear at this realization. He nods his head, seeming to understand, and gestures for me to follow him down a hallway. We walk in silence before he opens a door.

He's taken me to a library, or maybe actually it's more of a large office? Three walls are covered in floor-to-ceiling bookshelves. A large mahogany desk sits in the center with a matching chair tucked beside it.

"It's nothing fancy, but at least it's quiet." He gestures for me inside. "I'll be right outside, okay? Take all the time you need."

I throw my arms around him. He's stiff at first, not used to this kind of affection, but I don't care.

The door clicks quietly behind Marks, and I immediately begin exploring the room. I scan the books, lightly trailing my fingers along some of the spines. The shelves are filled with nonfiction titles, which is a bit disappointing. But honestly, what was I expecting? A historical Highlander romance tucked away on the shelves?

I continue reading the spines until I finally spot a familiar classic. With sudden determination, I wheel over the built-in ladder.

The book is more than halfway up the bookshelf, further proof that whoever's office this is—if it even is someone's office—definitely doesn't do much fictional reading.

I had misjudged where I placed the ladder, so I have to reach a bit for the book. I'm just shy of grabbing it, my fingertips brushing along the spine. Just a little further and I'll have it. I press one foot on the shelf, nearly dangling off the ladder as I reach for the book. No doubt, Marks would have a heart attack if he saw me right now.

As if Marks's sixth sense about me kicked in, I hear the door creak open. Knowing I'm caught red-handed, climbing these bookshelves like it's some jungle gym, I snap my attention toward the door, expecting Marks.

But it's Noah. The look of horror I imagined on Marks's face is now mirrored on Noah's face.

"Noah!" My surprise throws off my balance. I quickly move my foot, which was using the bookshelf for leverage, back to the ladder to try to right myself.

But somehow, my heel catches on a wooden step, making me lose my footing. I let out a shriek as I fall, closing my eyes for the rough landing that never comes.

I open my left eye, keeping my right squeezed shut as I assess my surroundings. Noah is looking down at me with a stunned expression, and I realize he's caught me.

Noah gives me a sad look. Or a pained one. Either way,

I don't like it. Especially because I'm the one who put it there.

Noah gently places me back on my feet and I look down at my dress, pretending to smooth out the fabric to give me a moment to collect myself.

"What brings you here, Agent Hart? Is there something I can help you with?" I nibble on my bottom lip anxiously as I turn back to him. I can't bring myself to look at his face, though, so I focus on his perfectly polished shoes. Because I know—I know if I looked at him, I'd throw myself into his arms.

He reaches his thumb out and gently pulls my bottom lip free from my teeth.

"Yeah, there is." His voice is gruff, and I hate the way it sends electricity throughout my veins.

He pauses, like he's waiting for me to look at him—and I reluctantly do.

"Call me Noah, please. I don't want to be Agent Hart with you."

"You came here to ask me to call you by your first name?" I ask, confused, because we both know that wasn't the real reason he came.

"I saw you run out, and then Marks told me you were in here. I can leave if you want to be alone." He takes a few steps back toward the door, and I glare at the space growing between us like I've been personally offended. Noah, of course, takes the glare as meant for him, nodding his head as he turns toward the door.

It's like I'm trapped in my nightmares—screaming at myself to move, but my feet won't budge. I can't speak or move; I'm just paralyzed as I watch him walk away.

"Say something, Ellie!"

"Oh, just one thing." He turns back around, standing in the open doorway. "I know I'm not in a position to ask for favors, but please, I beg you, don't ever climb on a bookshelf like that again." He reaches to close the door, and finally, I find my voice.

"How am I supposed to know that's even your real name? Everything about you was a lie!"

It's a low blow, I know. Not at all what I intended to say. I wanted to tell him not to go. I wanted to tell him I miss him. I wanted to tell him I can't stop thinking of him, that I think I'm in love with him.

In love with him? Ugh. I don't know. But what I do know that in such a short amount of time, he's become my favorite person. Well, after my platonic soulmate, Ollie, of course.

It's a feeling I've never experienced before. I've thought I'd been in love before, but this is different. This is all-consuming. This is so much more than anything I've felt before that I can't think it's anything but love.

"It wasn't," Noah responds, taking a small step back into the room. "Most things I told you were true. I do hate tomatoes, but love ketchup. My favorite era is Red. I… definitely don't know how to divide any number by seventeen, so that one was a lie, but I think you already knew that. My grandma really is in California, and my dad really is dead. He was an agent, actually—he died on duty."

He takes a few more steps towards me, the door closing behind him.

"That day on the river tubing? I told you I had jumped. I didn't just jump, though—I dove. I dove headfirst into my feelings for you. I'm in love with you, Ellie. Can't you see that?"

It comes out in a rush, like a confession he just has to get off his chest.

"If there's one thing you believe about me, believe that."

"What did you say?"

It's barely audible—I'm not sure I even said it out loud. He's in love with me?

"I was hired to protect the President of the United States and his family. Your dad had concerns that his daughter might try to make a break for it with her best friend at the gala—something they often attempted when together. Undercover agents were placed strategically at the gala and surrounding locations, but then there I was with the First Daughter, begging me to take the catering van. I realized you were going to take it with or without me, so it was going to have to be with.

"Your small taste of freedom as we drove away from that gala was electrifying. I wish you could have seen your face. Your smile was so wide, I wanted you to keep it a little longer.

"At my house, when you guys got the idea to take your road trip, I quickly consulted your dad, who decided you were going to keep chasing freedom, so you might as well do it, without realizing you were being protected and followed. Yes, I kept your father, Marks, and Ollie's security up to date on our whereabouts. They continued to catch up to us at our detours, still hoping to put an end to the cross-country trip despite all the measures in place. Plus, the Queen really did not like the idea—protection or not—that the heir to the throne was out on the open road.

"I started that trip to watch and protect Eleanor, but found myself falling more and more in love with Ellie.

"Across the room or across the world, I'd follow you. Not because I'm paid to, but because I want to. Because I want to be wherever you are."

My breath hitches, and I wish my body could understand the difference between Noah looking at me and jumping off a cliff. I try to take a steadying breath.

I don't hesitate. I don't even think as I rush toward him, quickly closing the distance between us and flinging myself into his arms, knowing he'll catch me, which, of course, he does with ease.

"I will do absolutely anything and everything to earn your forgiveness for not knowing who I was, for betraying your trust." He runs a few fingers through a strand of hair before tucking it behind my ear.

He doesn't need to do anything to earn my forgiveness. My parents and Ollie were right—the only reason I had any of those moments was because of him. It would have been another failed jailbreak from the gala without him.

I take a step away from him, and his hands fall to his sides. He's laid his cards out and thinks I'm about to break him, which is crazy. Did I not just fling myself into his arms?

"I love tomatoes!" I nearly shout, wanting the look of disappointment he's trying to conceal to disappear. The confused look he gives me would make me laugh under normal circumstances, but instead, I just keep going.

"I also love watching trashy reality TV. I know it's trash, but I can't stop. My favorite era was Evermore, but I've realized it's recently become Reputation." I give a half shrug.

"You know, there's love. There's angst. Exactly what you've brought into my life."

I wrap my arms around his neck. He looks at me with such hope, as if he understands I'm forgiving him. I take his face in my hands, gently rubbing my thumbs along his cheeks, hardly believing he's real.

He's real, and he loves me back. I know for certain I'm the luckiest girl to have someone like him love me.

"Noah, no matter how much I've tried not to be, I think…" I trail off and shake my head, looking away briefly before meeting his gaze again. "No, I know I'm in love with you."

Noah's face briefly flashes with what I guess is surprise, but I don't have time to read into it before his mouth crashes down on mine.

There are no fireworks exploding or stars twinkling above as we sit in a small-town parking lot. It's just us—

quiet and steady in this empty office. Despite no complaints about our previous kisses, this one is perfect. It's not some grand cinematic moment, but it's ours. It says everything I haven't been able to say. It conveys how much I've missed him, how I've fallen in love with him. How, to me, this is the real thing. It's not a fleeting moment or a holiday fling. He isn't some bittersweet memory I'll pack away. I've let others dictate what I do and where I go for too long, and I'm finally taking the reins of my own life.

Where do I start? Well, for one, by starting fashion design school. Second, by having Noah by my side from now on, no titles and no more secrets. Just the two of us.

I'd started to feel like I'd lost my identity in the midst of my title, but I'm beginning to see my future paved by Ellie and not Eleanor Hastings. I couldn't be more excited for what's to come.

Epilogue

The glittering lights of the ballroom blur together. The echoing sounds of clinking champagne glasses and waves of laughter die down as Dad steps up to a podium to say a few words.

I stand beside him, along with Mom and Grant, on stage at one of the many stops for his inauguration celebration. He won the reelection, which means another four years as the First Daughter.

I don't mind so much this time.

Because while Dad thanks those in attendance, my eyes drift to the man standing just offstage. He stands close enough, though, that I could reach out and touch him. He's not working tonight, but you'd never know it. His eyes continuously scan the room, searching for any sign of a threat.

Dad wraps up his speech, and I quickly turn my attention back to the guests, waving to the nameless faces who go back to celebrating Dad's victory. Noah's hand finds mine without even looking, his eyes remaining on the crowd. I take his hand and lead him behind the stage curtain, his eyes finally meeting mine.

"Hi." He gives me a small smile.

"You know you're my date tonight, right?" I tease. "You can turn off Secret Service mode."

He shakes his head as he pulls me towards him, wrapping his arms around my waist. "I know, I'm sorry. I just…I can't help it. I don't want to let my guard down. Not when it comes to you."

He leans down and lightly brushes his lips against mine. I don't let him pull away as I kiss him back, winding my arms around his neck.

A throat clears and we both look towards the curtain where Ollie has his head poking in, watching us with feign disgust.

"Can you two stop snogging for three seconds?" He grumbles. "Come on, I'm bored out here. My mum only let me come on behalf of the Crown *if* I was drowning in a security entourage. And they don't talk."

He opens the curtain wider to reveal a stone-faced man standing nearby on watch.

I laugh and drop my hands from Noah's neck. "Tell me about it. Security barely leaves me alone anymore."

"Yeah, well, yours seems a little more…voluntary," Ollie says, eyeing Noah. "You don't see *me* making out with anyone on my detail."

"True," I reply, grinning as I lace my fingers with Noah's. "Turns out I've become quite fond of mine.

Ollie groans. "Okay, okay, I get it. Come on, I came over here to escape the awkward silence, not walk straight into a Hallmark movie."

"Fine, see if you get to come to California with us in the morning."

Ollie stands up straight, his expression one of a scolded toddler. "What? No! I have to ride a mountain in space!"

It took a lot of convincing, begging, and contractual agreements, but our parents are finally letting us go to our final destination of our road trip. With very strict conditions.

We're to have a full security team. Keep our phones on, location sharing active. No arguing with Marks or Ollie's head of security. If they say no, it's no. Period.

I definitely tuned out the rest. Honestly, they could assign a personal drone to hover over my head, and surprisingly, I wouldn't care. All that matters is that I get a few days in California with Noah and Ollie. We'll see the Pacific Ocean. Ride Space Mountain. Eat churros under Disneyland fireworks. And then, while Ollie heads back across the pond, Noah and I—plus my charming fleet of bodyguards—will go visit his grandma.

I can tell he's nervous. But I'm not. I'm actually quite excited that I get to meet someone who's part of his story.

Even if it's not the chosen family I've already come to know. It was quite the surprise when I found out that Sawyer is actually in the FBI and Leah works at the Capitol. No wonder Ollie and I got away with spending the night at their place; they've already had some serious background checks.

"Come on," Noah tugs me back into the main room.

"I've seen you dance with far too many guys at these events; it's time for my turn."

Noah leads me to the dance floor, pulling me into the very center. He places a hand on my waist and pulls me close, his other hand held firmly in mine as a dreamy ballad plays softly across the room.

"You know, if it makes you feel any better, you were the first guy I danced with in a barn."

Noah laughs softly, the sound vibrating through his chest beneath my cheek.

"Did I mention how absolutely beautiful you are?"

I tilt my head up to look at him with a smile. "Hmm. Tonight or, like…ever?"

"Both."

"Yeah," I say, pretending to think. "You might have mentioned it once or twice…in the past twenty minutes alone."

Noah gently frames my face with his hands, smiling like I'm his entire world. "And did I mention how much I'm in love with you?"

"In love with me?" I pause like I'm thinking this one over as well. "Yeah, that one is ringing a bell."

"That's not good enough," he teases. "See, I need you to be absolutely certain."

He leans down and kisses me, soft and slow. I rise up on my toes, despite my heels, to deepen the kiss. The clattering of utensils and hum of voices eventually pull us apart, reminding us we're definitely not alone.

"You really have to stop doing that so shortly after I apply my lipstick." I swipe my thumb gently across his lips, wiping off any lipstick remnants.

"Never," he whispers, placing a quick kiss on my temple and guiding us back into the dance.

Only a few songs later, Grant weaves through the dancing couples to reach us in the center of the floor.

"Ellie, we're heading to the next party in a few moments."

I let out a small groan as Grant walks away, resting my forehead against Noah's chest.

"I'm partied out."

Noah chuckles and places a gentle kiss on the top of my head as we wander over to where Sawyer and Leah are chatting. I scan the crowd and spot Ollie flirting with a server. Typical.

I wave him to come over. Ollie's tagging along to each of the parties, too, which, to be fair, he loves.

"Honestly," I tease once he joins us, "you wonder why that memoir called you a ladies' man?"

"Too soon, Els, too soon." He says, wagging a finger at me. But he's smiling.

Turns out, the memoir had a lot of press leading up to the release, but once it was released, some super fans of the Royals started picking out inconsistencies. Pretty soon, the only chatter about the memoir was its credibility. And then, shortly after the release, Ollie got his (horrible) wish of something tragic to take over the news cycle when there was a hostage situation in London. Suddenly, all the BBC was talking about was uncovering any details about the hostage situation, dominating the news cycle, and any talk of the memoir quickly fizzled.

I nudge Ollie with my shoulder, and he bumps mine back, grinning.

"So, what's your plan, man?" Sawyer asks Noah. "You coming with us?"

Noah doesn't hesitate as he shakes his head and squeezes my hand. "I go where she goes."

And he does.

Not because he has to. But because he wants to.

And I wouldn't have it any other way.

Acknowledgements

Mom and Dad, per usual you do nothing short of support me. From Mom buying extra copies "just in case" she needs to give them to someone and Dad reading my book which was possibly his first book since elementary school (just kidding….kind of?)

Courtnie, Cami, and Darci for being my other biggest cheerleaders and acting interested in my writing even if they secretly are not in the slightest. (Okay, I think they actually are).

Dillon. You get your own shout out because you wanted to prove me wrong on my Becoming Cinderella acknowledgments and read it. So, shout out to you for that!

My seven nieces and nephews because you know, they're still my favorite people in the world. Apparently, the highest compliment for your generation is "slay!" So, you all "slay" (now please don't think I'm the uncool aunt for saying that).

Sara and Kiley for always hearing about every little detail through the journey of writing a book. (Also, I feel Harrison gets a shout out too for trying to push my book in Amsterdam!)

Stevie for your Stevie-isms. I told you I HAD to put bleeding like a hawk in a story and it's never not funny to me. Truly just another thing only we would find funny.

Kristen. What are the chances standing by you in line would take us where we are now? I love our talks about our current writings and appreciate your encouraging words (and letters).

Lindsey for basically being my unpaid PR agent. She always gets the cutest promo photos for me. She's so creative and if you've ever seen any of the pictures on my Instagram–that's all her.

To my gem of an editor, Grace. She really helped shape this story into what it is today and I am so grateful for her and her hard work.

To Ivanna for designing my cover because HELLO? Obsessed. Hang it in the Louvre.

Taylor Swift, because duh.

To all my extended family and friends who have been so supportive of my writing. I truly appreciate all the kind notes and comments and I feel so fortunate to have such a supportive group of people in my life!

And of course, to the readers. I am so appreciative to you for adding my stories to your TBR's. Thank you for even just a moment jumping into these worlds I create.

About the Author

Madison Packer graduated from Utah Valley University with a degree in English and a lifelong love of storytelling. When she's not reading or writing, she's probably rewatching *New Girl* or planning her next visit to a Disney park.

You can follow her on Instagram at @madisonpackerbooks.